Please Handle Me Carefully
For I Have Been

BROKEN

FLABIA THEMBEKA

INK START MEDIA
265 Eastchester Dr Ste 133 #102
High Point NC 27262

Please Handle Me Carefully For I Have Been BROKEN

FLABIA THEMBEKA

Table of Contents

Introduction 1

Dedication 2

Foreword 4

Rejection 6

Chapter One 18
Lena

Chapter Two 38
Craig

Chapter Three 52
Susan

Chapter Four 62
Alex

Chapter Five 84
Valencia

Chapter Six 96
The Broken Vessel

Introduction

By Flabia Thembeka

First of all, I would like to say 'thank you' to the HOLY SPIRIT for giving me such a powerful and emotional project as this book, *Please Handle Me Carefully, For I Have Been Broken*. This book is a much-needed resource and teaching tool to help aid all (and I mean *all*) those who have dealt with and had to endure the awful spirit of rejection in secret and, or in silence. To show them once and for all that there is a way of escape, in and through JESUS CHRIST, and that with HIM you can overcome this dreadful and devastating spirit and, yes, become whole. JESUS said in John 10:10, "The thief (satan) cometh not, but for to steal, and to kill, and to destroy: I am (JESUS) come that they might have life, and that they might have it more abundantly."

All the scriptures found in this book are from the authorized King James Version (KJV).

The stories and the lives of the five characters in this book are based on real people. Each has chosen to deal with the spirit of rejection in his or her own way. Each character came to be as a result of a difficult time in the lives of these people. They have had to endure and suffer from the spirit of rejection in secret or in the dark. Some of them have found the help that was needed to bring them into the light, and the others have continued on in darkness.

This spirit is one that has been sent from the enemy of your soul; his name is satan. Now, I know that the first letter of the name or word 'satan' should be capitalized; that would be editorially correct. But for me, it would be a slap in my face, as well as in the faces of all of those who have had to endure any or all of the many wicked and evil things that satan has inflicted on our lives. I will never, ever give satan any glory, nor will there be any acknowledgement of him. I don't intend for him to get any top billing in this book.

Satan is defeated, for his time is winding up and he knows it. To all of you, *Please Handle Me Carefully, For I Have Been Broken* will take you on a final healing journey, so that you may experience the love, freedom, and the healing that GOD has made available to you, once and for all.

Dedication

First, I would like to dedicate this book to the HOLY TRIUNE, because it is truly in you that I live, move, and have my being. Had it not been for You, I wouldn't be here. To 'my JESUS,' I love You so much for all that you did for me on Calvary and in YOUR resurrection. It is in YOU that we can all rise up and live again for real.

To my best friend, the HOLY SPIRIT, thank you so much for entrusting me with such a valuable project as this, and for giving me wisdom and understanding on such a delicate subject matter as this.

To the late Pastor James E. Watson, for showing me that as a mortal man, the greatest example of the man JESUS CHRIST, in the Earthly realm.

To Pastor Yohannah Watson, mere words cannot express how much I love and honor you as my pastor. I am truly grateful to the LORD JESUS for the spiritual and natural insight that HE has given you.

You stood firmly in your faith in Jesus Christ, while staring down the barrels of persecution and rejection. You stood as a pillar of strength and a beacon of light to all that were looking for the truth. You taught us to trust in GOD's WORD. You never wavered in your faith in the true and living GOD. Even today and in this hour you are still standing and encouraging others.

Pastor Yohannah, you're not only teaching them, but you're showing them through your walk with and in CHRIST. Always reiterating that no matter what they have to face; that it's truly worth having the LORD in their lives.

Pastor Yohannah, may you continue your journey always in the love of our Heavenly FATHER. It is through HIM that we all truly live, move, and have our being.

Foreword

By Pastor Yohannah Watson

Rejection is not a subject that's readily addressed in the Christian community yet is very prevalent. Many individuals have been told in their lifetime that they aren't good enough, that they are unwanted, or that they have no purpose in life, all of which are untruths. Over a period of time, they tend to believe the lies.

You will come to realize as you begin to read this book, which Ms. Thembeka has so informatively written, that the spirit of rejection is a spirit—one that takes on a life of its own in destroying the lives of others.

In traveling through the lives of Ms. Thembeka's fictionalized characters, you may recognize yourself or someone you may know. In doing so, don't be discouraged and think that there's no way out, because as you continue reading, you will find that THERE IS.

Pastor Yohannah Watson The former Pastor,
Abundant Life Teaching Center
Harvey, Illinois

Rejection

R ejection is a terrible thing for a person to experience. Victims (those who have been or are being abused) try hard to please their rejector (the one who is rejecting them) to the point of losing themselves. The more love and affection they give to the perpetrator, the more abuse and rejection they receive. Feeling trapped, with nowhere to go and no one to turn to, causes a whirlwind of thoughts to invade their minds, like swirling muddy floodwaters from a broken dam, rushing to confuse their minds.

Filtering through the dark thoughts, they find themselves saying, "This is not supposed to be happening; I'm only a child." They are seeking and searching for love and affection, like a crying baby looking for nourishment, only to find themselves in yet another abusive relationship, one after another; I call it 'the revolving door syndrome.' Rejection touches and reaches all walks of life, no matter the color of your skin, your job (title or position), your financial status (wealthy or impoverished), and/or your religious or church affiliation. It (rejection) just wants to control your life, with or without your permission.

1. Challenges

Many victims of mental, physical, and sexual abuse have personality flaws. They seem to think abuse and rejection go together hand in hand and, in most cases, they do. Some victims develop an unhealthy sense of loyalty toward their abuser. They return to their abuser after reaching adulthood, still seeking love and acceptance, whether the abuser is a parent, a sibling, friends, spouse, significant other, or even a child of their own.

When some victims observe their abuser interacting with others with love, respect, and kindness they desire (wanting it so much that it hurts them in the very core of their souls) to be treated in the same manner, as others are. However, this is not the case, so when they don't receive what they feel is rightfully due to them, their personality is altered. This altered personality is known as split personality or personality disorder. A victim who suffered from dramatic abuse explains his personality disorder as follows:

"As I seek the attention of my abuser, there is only one way for me to do it, and that's to split myself into many parts, be it two, ten, or more personalities. I only split when I'm rejected and feeling unloved. Many times, my personality changes without me knowing. In other words, I try to fight off offenses and not to allow them to affect me. But I don't always win.

"You see, there is a weariness that comes when this happens; a great fear of losing my mind comes over me. In fact, in my mind, I mentally battle to maintain my sanity. The fear of completely losing my mind and never being able to return back to normal haunts me."

2. Characteristics

From personal experiences, I know victims of abuse display one or the other or even both personalities' traits. They either behave very passive (like a child) or extremely aggressive and abusive (like their abuser). They are self-reliant (self-sufficient) and prideful (don't need or want help from anyone). When given a task or a challenge, the abused will usually accept it, no matter what it will cost them mentally, physically, or financially. They say, "I am strong, I can do anything, look at me, I am capable of doing and finishing the job or task."

Once the task is completed, however drained they may feel, they can now lie back and take a deep breath. Even if only for a moment, they can say within their hearts, "I did it, I can do it," all the while giving strength to the other, stronger personalities to protect the more inferior ones; the abused call this 'protecting myself at all cost.'

Whenever their abuser displays affection toward others, they feel insecure (doubtful and jealous). Then they become critical and judgmental (finding fault or judging severely) of the one who is receiving what they desire or have desired from their abuser. They are often very apologetic (always saying that they are sorry) even when it isn't their fault. They live in denial (an allegation is false) when caught or suddenly confronted, saying things about the abuser or others. They suffer from loneliness (the fear of being alone and unloved); this causes them to become depressed (sad and gloomy; downcast). Sometimes, they go so far into this state of mind that, without treatment, they become suicidal, feeling there is no hope or a way out for them.

I was told by another sufferer of abuse:

"There are times when I see my abuser with others, giving them the attention that I have longed for, for what seems like an eternity. Those others are receiving it without any effort on their part. No matter how short or how long the (attention) time may be, I find that I began to compare myself with these people to see how, why, and what my abuser sees in them. More than that, why is my abuser with me when no one else is around to see her do what she does to me? Why am I invisible to my abuser until she has a need (sexual or physical) and she wants me to come running and act like it is a privilege to be in her presence, and is constantly telling me, 'So just be happy that I allowed you in my space,' which I usually am? I want to feel wanted by my abuser; I desire to be needed by her. I always apologize for not being there to fix things or to help her when she needs something. If my abuser has a bad day, I say I'm sorry, as if it were my fault. Someone has to take the blame for it, so why not me? At least my abuser is here with me right now. I just need someone, anyone, no matter how they (the abusers, present or past) treat me; just please take notice of me."

3. Treatments

The abused as well as their predators have a need to be made whole. There are so many abused and broken people in the world today and the numbers are still climbing every day. Most of them suffer in silence, and unfortunately, die in their very silence. They are growing tired of always putting on the many masks that they have made, of their own free will, to become part of their daily lives, (and they secretly swear by 'it') saying 'it' will serve to never to reveal who I really am, and they wear the masks every day to hide themselves.

This takes me back to a sermon illustration by the late Pastor James E. Watson. He was asking us, his congregation, "Can we all be real this morning?" He told us that GOD sees us no matter what we do or say, because HE sees us all the time. He said, "We can all pretend for a few hours on each Sunday." Then he said, "But we, the congregation, (as well as every one of you out there reading this) couldn't pretend with the people we live with and work with. What would the people at your various jobs say about you? If I told them that you were a Christian, would they laugh, or be shocked, or would they agree?" Then he asked us, "What if I asked your children how you are at home? Would they say you act like this all the time, or that you are just pretending for the rest of us here?" He then said, "Remember, every actor has to lay his part down sometime, and every clown has to take off his makeup. So can we all be real with one another this morning?" Then he asked us to do as he was about to do. Pastor Watson placed his hand under his chin as if to grip a mask and began to pull it over his head. He asked us, "Can we all just take off the masks and be real with ourselves and GOD for just a couple of hours?"

If we would come clean and really be real with ourselves, we would acknowledge that we are truly in need of some kind of help. Not the kind where we place a bandage over the wound and go on like nothing happened. We need to seek some real help, not only to keep it together for right now, but for always and forever.

Many abused people have sought out the different psychiatrists, psychics, readers, different religions, and even participated in an exorcism, all the time trying to find a remedy or a solution for what is really ailing them. Somehow, this didn't and doesn't help; for the most part, it just leaves them more confused and locked deeper into a more devastating state of mind, wondering if there is someone they can trust. "Will I ever find a way out of this horrific place that I am locked into without a key, a map, or just something or someone to steer me in the right direction?"

It seems like every time we gain the strength and/or the courage to seek out help, there is that voice again in our minds telling us that we can't escape the jaws of rejection and abuse.

Have you ever had a flat tire, and you didn't have a spare? Has your battery ever died for one reason or another? Has your car ever hit a very large pothole, and the whole front end landed in it? Have you ever had a blowout on the highway, or did your car just break down? How do you repair these things? We can fix a flat tire; we can even ask someone for a jump, or for the use of their jumper cables. For the things that we can't handle and that are out of our control, we can call for a tow service company.

But for the abused, it isn't that easy. It is a matter of life and death. Very often, more times than they can imagine, they have wrestled with the thought of getting help only to retreat, feeling that, "There really is no help for me." Besides that, you have to understand one thing: they are not crazy; they are trying *not* to crack up because of all the pain that they are in. They need a way out, to escape the pains of rejection and abuse that they feel, even if it is just to put a bandage on it for a few moments. This is part of their protection; they hide behind some kind of card, like they have a full deck of cards on the inside, and whichever one they feel at the time will overpower the abuse, is played, and 'it' will become their protector. They don't realize that they can never figure out what their 'real' opponent, satan, will do, or what satan has dealt or will deal out to them as their strength.

But it is not strength; it is a weakness. Say, for instance, you had an uncontrollable desire to eat ice cream, but in order for you get it you have to give away some of yourself, give something away to this enemy of your soul, then the ice cream will soothe your desire. But what did it cost you? It cost you part of yourself. There is always a trick or a test, but you don't have to give in and give yourself away piece by piece. The abused are always seeking love and acceptance, the kind that only GOD can give. If only the abused could or would accept the love, the healing, and the help that GOD has made readily available for them in HIS WORD. Through this process, the abused one can become whole for most of them, for the very first time in their lives. Even with this type of help readily available to them, they are not willing to receive the necessary help, or (physically as well as emotionally) are not able to receive it.

The abused never allow anyone in to see their real feelings, for fear that other people may find out that, "I am broken, and I'm not perfect," while trying to keep the pieces of their scattered lives seemingly together. They also have to face an even greater fear: knowing that they will eventually fall apart. They continue to rely on their many 'selves' to get them out of this or that situation or crisis. Whenever they feel they are being attacked, they use strong words to cause the person whom they feel threatened by to back down; they may even invite that individual to a fight. They must always come out on top, no matter the cost to themselves or others. It is a chance that they have to, and are willing to, take.

Sometimes they make a declaration in a loud voice that only they can hear: "I'm not broken; there's nothing wrong with me! I can make it. You just watch; I always land on my feet!" Then, with even a much louder cry on the inside, they say, "I'm strong, and nothing can hurt me!"

These are the cries and voices of the lonely rejected ones; unknowingly, they have just given the spirit of rejection a more powerful foothold over their lives. The abused feel like they are protecting themselves, but each time, they feel more and more rejected once again. They never realize that they are powerless against this hideous and horrid spirit of rejection. So, the abused find themselves going from the jaws and claws of one perpetrator to the next, not ever being able to control or resist the next abuser from entering their lives. The abused just stand there and roll out the welcome mat and say, "Come in, do whatever you want. I will receive you with my arms, my eyes, and my heart wide open." Like a magnet, they are drawn into yet another abusive relationship. Have you ever noticed that the rejected ones always find themselves right back in the same spot as before, only this time it's worse, much worse than ever before?

That is how the spirit of rejection operates; it causes the abused to give off that negative vibe that allows only another perpetrator (the next rejector) in a crowded place with hundreds of people to find and seek them out. However, for the abused, even in a crowded room, they can feel very lonely. With this frame of mind, the abused lead a very lonely life that often becomes unbearable for them. Often, they can become suicidal, and some even commit suicide, ending their internal pain once and for all.

Why don't the abused just cry out for help? It's because in the back of their mind, the first person who rejected them was a parent, or some other person who was very close to them. Weren't their love ones supposed to love and nurture them? Instead, the rejector used the power or authority that they had over the person in a negative way; instead of helping, loving, nurturing, directing, and protecting them, they abused them in one way or another. So how do the rejected look for or seek help? Do they even know, or better yet, do they realize that they need help even when CHRIST Himself is a part of their lives? They say, "How can CHRIST love me when my own parent(s) or the one who raised me didn't love me and rejected me? Why didn't they care for, protect, feed, and clothe me?" Yes, that is the role of the parent, but not all parents are role models. Most of them didn't have a good example to model themselves after. That's why there are so many broken homes, and where there is a broken home, you will find a lot of broken people.

Yes, some make it out and survive, but, what is the percentage? Only GOD knows. And what about those who don't? What about the ones who haven't even tried, or even have the desire to get help? Why would they, when their parents didn't get the help that they so desperately needed? And, most of them weren't ready to become parents themselves, either; they just got caught up in the moment. They never even received any help. So how do we, and why do we, expect them to be able to help us? They can only give us what is in them to give, whether it's love and comfort or hate, on all, and any level, and in any shape, form, or fashion. Hurt and abuse are truly all they really know and are able and trained to give. Do you expect to receive hot water from the faucet when you turned on the cold water handle? No; so do not forget you are talking about another abused person who has hated what happened to them; they are yet, even in this day and hour, and at this very moment, trying to hide under the radar from their abusive past, too. Rather than pouring out love and affection, they pour out hate and pain, the very same pain that is inside them. As crazy as it may seem or even sound, the perpetrator gets relief from his or her own pain by inflicting pain on others who are more helpless, and hopeless, than they are. This cycle has gone through generation after generation from the beginning of time. It is as if they are paying back the very same person, whoever it may have been, who abused them, never realizing that the one who abused them didn't have a clue about the damage that they inflicted; nor has it crossed their heart or mind. Nor do they even care; they just need to get some kind of relief from their pain. So if you are in their path, you will feel the brunt of their wrath, intentional or not. See, the perpetrator has vowed never to be abused again, or become a target for abuse. So they reverse the roles and find someone they can have control over, but not intentionally meaning to abuse them; it just happens that way. I cannot stress this any more than I have that it really is a spirit that is driving them, a spirit that is smarter and stronger than they are. And they have given themselves over to this spirit without ever being aware of it. Understand this: 'it' (the spirit of rejection) has been going through families for generations, destroying them.

Please allow me to give you an example: Have you ever seen a family where the grandparents drink? The children did pills, drugs that needed needles, and/or weed. Now their grandchildren are doing 'happy sticks,' coke or rocks and whatever the new fad or combination is the 'in' thing now. Remember that the abused and the abusers are one and the same. The abuser has just had all that they feel that they could possibly handle, stomach, or take from anyone else in this life, and only want to get revenge on the one who originally rejected them, the real perpetrator who started the terrible chain of events in their life. Unfortunately, this is some of what causes so many horrible crimes and acts against many helpless people. They are unaware of what was done to or has happened to them.

These people don't have CHRIST as the head of their lives, and they don't want and don't feel they need HIM. However, did you know that there is something even worse than that? There are so many of us who have already accepted CHRIST into our lives, but not HIS help to heal the many wounds and battle scars that every one of us had before we gave our lives over to HIM. This is why we who truly know the LORD JESUS CHRIST as our personal SAVIOR and DELIVERER must sincerely and whole-heartedly pray for those who need deliverance to be delivered and set totally free. Our hearts should go out to our sisters and brothers. We should be glad and feel that we are privileged that we are able to stand in the gap for them, seeing that someone else did it for you, and HIS name is JESUS CHRIST, and HE is interceding for *all* of mankind right at this very moment.

While reading this book, with all the different turns and places it will take you to, I don't mean or desire to give this spirit of rejection exposure, but to expose it fully so that people who are suffering from it will be set free.

4. Examples

Traits of one who has or is suffering from rejection:

*They are always trying to please their rejector.

*They suffer from split or multiple personalities.

*They have been abused one or more times.

*They feel rejection and abuse go together hand in hand.

*They have developed a sick sense of loyalty to their rejector (no matter who it is).

*They have a deep desire and longing to be treated with the same love and respect that is given to others by their rejector.

*The rejected must always apologize to the rejector even if they haven't done anything wrong. This is how they are made to feel that they never do anything right, at any time.

*The rejected have developed this wall of strength, so if there is a fear that they are being attacked, they will attack back with a vengeance, (meaning that one or more of these superior personalities will come out to save the inferior personality).

*They are controlling, and they look for their prey, their next victim, just like the rejector found them, in need of almost everything.

Traits of a Rejector:

Everything just as displayed by the rejected, above, only he or she has turned the tables on another who is weaker than they are.

Chapter One

Lena

*Lena is a fictional character; she has suffered abuse. There is a way
out for her and all those who are like her.*

Lena is a young woman, very beautiful, and her hair is jet-black and
wavy. Her eyes are a honey brown; she has beautiful white teeth, but
they are kind of small. Her skin is a yellowish brown and creamy,
with not a flaw in it anywhere, even after all she has gone through. Her smile
is a very genuine smile, if she smiles at all. She seems so sad most of the time
on account of her very hard existence from a very early age. Because of that,
she loves really hard, since she wasn't loved much in the past.

Now she's met a young man who is just dreamy, whom she feels is worthy
of her love and trust. He says all the right things, and he does everything
perfectly; always attentive to her needs, he even listens to her intensely. One
would think he really isn't for real, like that old saying, "If it's too good to
be true, it very well may be too good to be true."

Years ago, Lena decided to stop loving or trusting anymore, especially
since she had never received back what she gave out, never, ever really
understanding why, but always a person pleaser, even if it meant she would
do without. Most of the time, she spent her nights crying and wanting
to just give up and die, always wondering what the reason was for living.
She had had this thought more times than she'd cared to think of. She
was so afraid that she wasn't loveable or worthy to be loved. There were so
very many hurts and pains that sometimes, she could hardly get up in the
morning to face a new day.

Yet after all these years, she meets this guy, Craig. He seems nice enough,
and she has had her eye on him for a year or two. They finally meet at one
of the church socials for the first time; that is, for her and Craig. However,
this is the first time that they are introduced properly, even though they both
attend the same church. They have dinner together and talk the evening
away. Craig causes Lena to laugh a lot during dinner. He pays so much
attention to her and he really pays her a lot of compliments, as well.

As time would have it, they started dating, and then after only a short time, Lena and Craig became intimate. Lena was sore afraid because she really preferred to be married the next time that she took this step again. Yet because of the fear of losing this wonderful man, and not knowing how to tell him how she felt, she went along just to keep him. She knew that it was a big step to become so close to anyone. This could have led to an unwanted pregnancy like before (even though she couldn't help herself); it would be said that it was all her fault, and maybe that she was trying to entrap him. Then there was her faith, and that she knew that GOD honors intimacy only in marriage; other than that, it is a sin to be in a relationship of fornication. And yet she went along with it. She didn't want to lose Craig; besides, he was so sweet. She knew then that she was truly in love, and he was really the man for her.

Later on, after their first time, when she was all alone that evening, Lena felt very sad. She knew that she had hurt herself and GOD. But she had made her choice, to fall into the trap that the enemy set for her, yet she continued on with it anyway, knowing and thinking better. As she began speaking out loud to herself, she said, "How can this be so wrong when he makes me feel so good and warm inside, and Craig is so gentle with me?" And he even said that he loved her (not that he was in love with her; there is a big difference), doesn't that count for anything?

After a few of these steamy nights, Lena fell desperately in love with Craig, but these nights lasted for only a couple months. Now her darling Craig was no longer reachable. She couldn't understand. He was so sweet, lovable, understanding, easy to talk to, and was always bringing her a gift of some sort. From sending her beautiful flowers on the job, now he pretended that she was not there, or that she never meant anything to him.

Lena began to question herself, "What happened? He told me that he loved me; he even held me like he did."

One time, when she did get Craig on the phone, he said just to chill, he wasn't ready for a serious or a deep, lasting relationship. *But that's not how he made me feel or what he led me to believe. What went wrong? Can I fix it?* Now Craig was starting to say things like, "I don't know where I will be in five weeks," and more than that, he didn't have a clue as to where he would be in the next five or ten years. He said GOD hadn't shown him his life thus far, he just knew he was on the road with GOD and he was following Him. *Was he following GOD when he got me in the sack? In any case, he now just wants us to be friends; how do you go from being lovers to just friends? Friends don't have sex, do they?* That was all Lena could hear as she sat on her bed after she hung up the phone from talking to Craig. *When he told me that he loved me, was it just a lie just to get where he really wanted to be?* Or was it that, secretly, she did really want to be wanted by a man and that she was willing to believe just about anything? For just once in her life, she wanted to believe that she had felt loved—or had she?

Maybe she should take a chance this one time, even with her deep, hidden fear, the fear that told her that she was missing out on life, and that it would just pass her by. Would she ever get a chance at love again if she had said no to Craig?

Now, Lena has become withdrawn, feeling unattractive, lonely, and rejected once again, since her breakup with Craig. With all these new and some of her old mixed emotions, she tries to face life. Going to work and to church with her head held down, thinking only of Craig and their 'brief encounter;' that is what he now calls it. Now, she must cope with her feelings, still fantasizing about being married to him, not wanting it to be over; but it *was* over as far as Craig is concerned. She picks up the phone to call him again, only to get voicemail telling her to leave a message, and she has already left several of them, with not one single response from Craig. Lena's heart is telling her Craig didn't really mean what he said to her. *Maybe it was something I said or did wrong,* Lena thinks, *maybe there is something that I can say or undo to change Craig's heart and mind about me.* She had Craig in love with her once; he could fall for her again. Maybe, Lena could get Craig back there to the way they were before all of this. And then Craig would come to his senses and realize that he really, truly loves her, and then they can be married.

Who is Lena fooling? No one but herself. Craig has moved on and doesn't plan on coming back to her ever.

This is the way Lena's life has been all of her young life, one rejection after another. Never feeling wanted or needed, not even by her own family. Lena had been repeatedly raped and molested by her mother's live-in friend; that all started from the time that Lena turned four years old. She started to withdraw on the inside, when she couldn't protect herself from her attacker and his many threats against her mother and her twin brothers. He always told Lena that she would come home one day from school and they would all be dead. And it would be all her fault for telling their secret.

Other times, as she began to get older, he would call her horrible names and tell her that no one would ever believe her, all the while saying that she was a little liar. Explaining to Lena that it was her, all the time, who wanted to do this and went after him in the first place. Then he would, in turn, tell everyone that she was a liar and he knew for sure everyone would believe him, especially since he was really a nice guy to everyone else. Lena was always afraid for her family, yet hurting and afraid of what was happening to her. All the time she wondered, "Is it ever going to come to an end at some point in my life?" Still always being so afraid, she went along with her attacker. He stopped only because she became pregnant and began to show. She was so scared and frightened out of her mind, fourteen and pregnant.

What was she to do? So she decided to tell her mother what had been going on all those years with her mother's friend, and her mother didn't believe her, and she took his side. She kicked Lena out of the house and into the streets, pregnant, with no place to go and no one to turn to. Her mother's friend had alienated them from the rest of their family, so Lena didn't know them or where they lived or how to search for them. What was she to do, now that she was out on the streets on her own?

She'd been out there for two and half days, hungry, tired, and sleepy. She started blaming herself for not speaking up sooner; maybe her mom might have believed her and not her lying friend. With no help or support, Lena remembered it was only a few days ago that she was at home and she had a warm dry bed. How could her mom just kick her out into the streets? "Doesn't she even care where I am or of what has become of me? No, she called me some horrible names too, all the while telling me to get my lying behind out of her house. Telling me at the same time, 'You are a disgrace,' and I'd get what was coming to me and that she never wanted to see me ever again." Now Lena starts to think, did her mom ever love her, did she want her, or has she always been looking for a way to get rid of her? How can she sleep and rest, knowing that her daughter's out there on the streets with no place to go?

This was what happened to Lena. No one believed her, and she was the only one telling the truth. Her mother's friend, he turned it all around to be Lena's fault, and made her out to be a tramp. He said some of his buddy's sons said that they had been with Lena and more than once, and that every boy on the block had had his way with her. That wasn't the truth; only he and Lena knew what the real truth was, that he had been having her since she was four, and ten years later, she was pregnant with his baby. Lena prayed that one day he would get what was coming to him for all the things he had done to her and all the years he did them.

Finally, Lena found a nearby shelter after being on the streets for a few days. Lena decided to go to this shelter around the corner from the alley that she had been sleeping in, only to end up raped and beaten during the night. This beating put her in the hospital with a miscarriage, and with a hospital stay of about a month. The hospital administration tried to get a few of her family's names out of her, but she told them that they were dead and that she was all alone. In the hospital, she ate three meals a day. But when she got wind that they were going to put her in a foster home, she left the hospital without a word.

With no place to go, Lena was back on the streets again. Now she had to try to figure out how to survive on the streets; she couldn't take another beating like that. She was too young to go on welfare or to get a job; besides, who would hire her with no work experience and the way she looked? She was dirty and hungry. So she started begging and asking for handouts wherever she could get one. There were not a lot of people out there on those streets who would help; some were nice and kind, like this guy she met. He said he helped a lot of girls, and he had a place where she could sleep and eat and get plenty of rest. (Now, you know that he was lying through those gold teeth of his.) But Lena found this out a little too late in the game of life. Before long, he put her to work on the streets, to pay for her room and board. After being out there so many months, Lena became numb to the name-calling, the beatings, and all the nasty acts. Really, it was just all the things a child had to learn to put up with when she was on the streets.

One day, this nice old lady came around the spot where Lena worked, and she began telling her about GOD and that GOD loved her. Lena told the lady that if GOD really loved her, where had HE been all this time and where was HE when she needed HIS help? Lena loved her mom, but she really didn't care about Lena. "After all, she kicked me out into the streets. She was supposed to love and protect me, but she didn't do either one. And through all the abuse that I suffered at home, I was trying to protect them, and they turned on me, so why and how could GOD love me?"

The lady finally gave Lena a tract to read on John 3:16. Then she gave her a note, folded up very small, with her phone number on it. She told Lena if she ever got tired of this life, if she needed anything, or just a place to rest, please give her a call. No strings attached. On the streets, everyone learned not to trust anyone and to be very skeptical of people; no one ever gave anybody anything for free. So what was this old lady's game? They all had a game; was she some kind of freak? Maybe she liked young girls, yet Lena could see the kindness in her eyes, the kind she had seen years ago.

She began reminiscing about an old mother at the church she had gone to with her grandma. The lady used to hug and hold her all the time while telling her, "JESUS loves you so much," and at other times, she would hold Lena and say, "GOD loves you, baby." That was back when Lena was eight and a half years old; her grandma was a sweet old soul, and the only one who Lena really felt loved and safe around. Lena never dared tell her grandmother about the sexual abuse that she was dealing with at home, because she thought it would kill her, but her grandma died anyway. At her grandma's church, the people were genuine, and if they told you they loved you, they meant it. They were not flakey like the people she encountered these days.

While Lena was in deep thought, she felt a pain in her heart because she was missing her grandma so much. "Maybe if she were alive today, I wouldn't be on the streets." When Lena looked up, the old lady was gone. Then she thought to herself, *maybe one day I will give that old lady a chance to prove herself, maybe she really does mean well. But I will watch her closely and very carefully. I know that I will have to watch what I say around her, just so she won't be able to use it on me later. Well, nothing is going on out here, and my feet are so tired, but I don't know if I'm ready to go back to that old dump I live in. Maybe I will give that old lady a call from the phone in the hallway outside of my room.*

Once inside her room, Lena took a much-needed shower. As she was picking up her things, she saw that the note that old lady had given her earlier had dropped on the floor. Lena read the note. It said, "My name is Mother Burns," and Lena laughed to herself. *Huh, I've been burned a lot of times but never by anyone whose name is 'Burns'.* Lena sat down on her cot, thinking about how tired she was and how tired she was of the life that she was living. She'd been on the streets for five very long years. Lena began to wonder that maybe Mother Burns had something that she could use.

After some time, Lena went to call Mother Burns, first, checking to see if the hallway was clear before she opened her door. It was clear. Now, the next most important thing she had to do she had to make sure there was no one around, because some people, like her pimp, had eyes and ears everywhere. So Lena walked over to the phone, dropped the coin in the slot, dialed the number, and waited. While she was waiting for it to ring, she began to chicken out, but before she could hang up, Mother Burns was already saying, "Hello, hello, is anyone there?" She had such a sweet and soft voice, but Lena hung up anyway. Lena went back to her gloomy and not well-lit apartment; no matter how it looked, it was hers, and no one was going to put her out ever again. Lena began to cry, thinking about her past, but she soon fell asleep; she was so very tired.

Round about two in the morning Lena was awakened by some very loud shouting, and gunshots. Lena immediately rolled off her cot onto the floor and crawled to the window. Lena wanted to see if she could see what was happening and also make sure that she was not seen by the people below. But, the rooming house had a lighted *Vacancy* sign hanging right outside her window, and it was flashing, as it always did, all day and all night. She feared that she might have been spotted by one of the shooters, because she heard one of them ask the other, "Did you see someone in that window with the sign?" By the time the other guy looked up, Lena had already slid down onto the floor, and she began crying because she was so afraid; she knew if they did see her, she was as good as dead. Lena started to think fast. She had to get out of there to somewhere safe.

Suddenly, she started throwing all the things that she could carry into a couple of plastic bags and the one large brown paper bag that she had in her room.

She decided now was the time to call the 'Burns' lady, but not here; she had to get as far away from this place as she could. Lena needed a safe place to call from, where no one knew her, and just maybe she could stay there and lie low until everything blew over. "I'll call that 'Burns' lady when I get somewhere safe, far from here."

Lena began running as fast as she could, in the direction of town where she thought no one knew her. Especially away from the men with the guns. After a long while, she began to get tired of running. Still running, but a bit slower, she spotted a telephone booth. Then, Lena knew that it was time and she needed to stop running, so she stopped at the phone booth and called the Burns lady. This time, the phone rang only once, and she heard that same soft and kind voice once again.

"Hello, hello, is anyone there?"

Lena was ready to hang up, but she couldn't because she could hear Ms. Burns still talking.

"Is everything all right? Do you need help? Are you somewhere safe? Talk to me, I will be glad to come and get you. Are you still there?"

Finally, Lena spoke up, saying, "It's me. This is Lena. You told me if I ever needed any help or anything, that I could call you, right?"

Then Ms. Burns asked, "Is everything okay?"

Before answering her, Lena quickly decided to take a quick look around at her surroundings. Once she had done that, she answered Ms. Burns, saying that she wasn't sure, but she thought that she was for the moment. So Ms. Burns asked Lena for the address where she was, so that she could come get her. Ms. Burns wrote it down: 1210 Longwillow Drive. She told Lena that she knew where it was, and she would be there in about ten minutes, but if she was just a little late, to please stay there and wait for her.

While Lena was waiting for her to arrive, she began thinking back about how life was before, but before she could really get into thinking about it any further, she heard a car horn. When she looked around to see who it was, she realized it was Ms. Burns blowing for her.

"Come on," Ms. Burns said. "Let's go for some coffee and donuts, or tea if that's what you like, come on and get in."

After Lena got in the car, Ms. Burns told Lena that she knew a diner that was open twenty-four hours. Then Ms. Burns drove to the Iron Skillet Diner, where they ate some food and talked a lot.

Mother Burns, as she was called by those who knew and loved her, all throughout their conversation while she was talking to Lena, kept telling her how much GOD loved her. The only thing Lena thought was, *She doesn't even know me or what I've done or where I come from; how can she or GOD love me? If she only knew, I wonder what she would say then, when or if she finds out. I bet that will change her heart and mind about people like me. And one thing is for sure, if GOD is really who Mother Burns says HE is, HE has already given up on me and everyone like me. But HE doesn't like it when we sin or act bad, as my grandmother would always say when she caught me acting up. I really hated that, especially when she said it and spanked me, too. Huh, those really were the good old days at grandma's house.*

"Honey, are you listening?" Mother Burns asked. "JESUS does love you, and that is why HE died just for you and me and everyone else."

As Lena continued to listen and to talk with Mother Burns, Lena found herself crying a lot, thinking about all past hurts and pains of her life. Ms. Burns told Lena that tears were for helping to relieve some of the pressure that everyone felt on the inside. Lena thought, *You know, no matter what I say, Ms. Burns' response to me would be, 'GOD really loves you, baby.'* Ms. Burns took her Bible out and read John 3:16. After Ms. Burns read it, Lena thought, *GOD really does love me.* Ms. Burns told Lena about the enemy (satan) who was the source behind all Lena's hurt and the pain in Lena's life, and that satan's job was to kill, steal, and destroy lives. Ms. Burns said that satan didn't want anyone to find out about JESUS and all that HE had done for people, and Ms. Burns said JESUS did it all because HE loves Lena. Then Ms. Burns told Lena satan didn't want her to give her life to JESUS.

As they sat there, Mother Burns went through so many Scriptures with Lena that they didn't even notice it was daybreak outside. She wanted to make sure that Lena knew all that JESUS had done for her. Also, that HE loved and will always love her, even if she never in turn loved HIM. Then she said she was getting tired and needed to get some kind of rest before it got too much lighter outside. She offered to take Lena to a family member or friend's house, but she told Mother Burns that she didn't have either. She said if Lena didn't mind being in a small, quiet place, that she could get some rest at her house. So Lena went with her.

When Lena got there, she found that it wasn't as Mother Burns had described; it was a good-sized place with two bedrooms, and both were a nice size. There was a large dining room, a full eat-in kitchen, and a decent-sized bathroom with a bath and shower, and it felt so warm and cozy in her home. The spare bedroom was where she said Lena could stay. It was just beautiful; it had a twin bed, a dresser, a nightstand with a lamp and Bible on it, and it had a closet, too. Lena hadn't felt this welcome in any place since the times that she stayed at her grandma's house. That all ended when her grandma died. While Lena was thinking to herself, she was looking around, trying to take everything in as fast as she could without making Mother Burns aware of what she was doing. Mother Burns went into the dresser and pulled out some pajamas for Lena to sleep in. Then Ms. Burns told Lena that she was welcome to go take a bath or shower and relax, so that her body could get some good, well-needed rest. Once Lena got out of the tub and into those pajamas, and got into bed, she fell fast asleep before her head had a chance to hit the pillow good.

When she awakened around two o'clock that afternoon, it was the smell of food cooking which had awakened her. It smelled like her grandma's cooking, and she had been a really good cook, too. Then she noticed that all her clothes had been washed and ironed and were lying there at the foot of the bed all very neat. She got up, got dressed, made up the bed, then went to the kitchen, and there was Mother Burns singing a hymn and cooking up a storm. She said that she liked cooking, but there was no one to cook for anymore. Her husband had died a few years back, and they'd never had any children, and they were their parents' only children. When they had gotten married, they wanted to have a big family, but it didn't happen the way they had planned. So for forty-five years, they had each other. But Mother Burns explained to Lena about her having such a wonderful church family, and how she got to cook for some of the many functions, and by doing that, she felt useful and a part of a larger family. So she asked if Lena was hungry, and Lena said that she was, so Mother Burns said, "Have a sit, and I will fix you a plate." She really had done some cooking: there were greens, yams, macaroni and cheese, corn bread, and fried chicken. Lena thought she had died and gone to heaven, oh boy, was the food good! After they ate, Lena helped her wash the dishes and clean up the kitchen.

After a few days of being at Mother Burns', Lena felt rested and kind of different; she really couldn't explain it. She noticed that Mother Burns was always smiling and humming some kind of song, and the sound of it was always soft and pleasant. One day, she asked Mother Burns how she came to be at such peace. She told Lena that many years ago, she had accepted JESUS CHRIST as her LORD and SAVIOR, and HE was the one who made every day worth facing with joy in her heart. And no matter whether her days were good or bad, she didn't have to face them alone, "Because HE is always right here with me to help in every situation." She said this was why her life was fulfilled and worth living. This was why she always desired to share HIS love with others; maybe she'd be able give out some of what HE had given and shown her through HIS undying love. This was why she told others about JESUS. So Lena asked her how she could feel the way Mother Burns did. She told Lena to go get the Bible off the nightstand and she would show her. When Lena gave her the Bible, she turned it to Romans 10:9-10, asked her to repeat the words with her, and Lena did. "That if thou shalt confess with thy mouth the Lord Jesus, and shalt believe in thine heart that God hath raised Him from the dead, thou shalt be saved. For with the heart man believeth unto righteousness; and with the mouth confession is made unto salvation." Then Mother Burns said Lena had just done what it took to be saved, and she was now saved.

Now Lena was a follower of CHRIST, and JESUS was now LORD

over her soul. Mother Burns asked her if she believed it, and Lena said that she did, but she still didn't feel like all that singing and stuff, like Mother Burns did. She began to laugh and said, "It will all come in due time, and when it does, you will want everyone to know." Then she told Lena that as she began to read her Bible each day, she would begin to change from the inside out, because GOD's WORD is cleansing, and it repairs people day by day as they allow HIM to do it.

Lena started going to church with Mother Burns sometimes in the evenings at The Little Lighthouse Mission Church. The people there were very nice people, and she noticed that there were a lot of young people like her at the church, which made her feel good that she wasn't the only one. She and Mother Burns went to Bible class in the evenings on Wednesdays, and two services on Sunday, which Lena really enjoyed a lot. And no one looked down on her or asked her any questions about her past; they just gave her hugs like they did for everyone else.

One day, Lena told Mother Burns that she was ready to start the deeper healing process in her life. She longed to see her two younger brothers, the twins Joshua and James. They probably didn't even know what had happened to her, well, the real truth anyway. They were the only family that she had, outside of her mother. But, that meant calling her mother and telling her that Lena had forgiven her for how she had treated Lena. She then called the last phone number she had for her mother, but someone Lena didn't know answered the phone. Still, Lena asked the person on the other end of the telephone line if she could to speak to her mother. Lena was told that her family didn't live there anymore and that they, the new tenants, had had this number for the last four years. So Lena asked the lady on the other end of the telephone if she knew anything about her family and, or where they had moved to. But the lady was able to tell Lena only what she had heard or been told by other people. The lady told Lena that her mother had died at the hand of her boyfriend while trying to protect one of Lena's brothers from him. And he was now serving life in the state penitentiary. She also told Lena her two brothers were now in the system.

Lena is now twenty-two years old and has been saved for a little better than two and a half years. Loving and learning of the LORD, she prays for her brothers each day, and she asks GOD to save them just as HE had saved her. Then she asks HIM to help her to find them someday.

When she finally talks to Mother Burns about what had happened to her mother and brothers, Mother Burns says she will try to help find them. Nowadays, Lena works at a grocery store on the corner as a cashier. Her boss, Mr. Scott, is a very nice Christian man; he is a serious businessman, but he is fair. He's never tried to make a pass at her, nor has he ever said anything out of the way to her. He says that she is like part of his family. Mr. Scott is like the neighborhood's uncle to everyone, but he doesn't allow anyone hanging outside in front of his store. The store is a clean and safe place to work. Each day before the store is opened for business, Mr. Scott has a word of prayer; he always thanks GOD for the day, and then he asks for protection for everyone throughout the day.

At church, everyone is all excited about the up-and-coming big church social, and it is just a few weeks away. Lena has already been asked to the church social by a couple of the young men. However, Lena is still debating on whether she will be able to attend. She, really doesn't know or have an idea of what to say, do, or anything, and more than that, what to wear to an event like this. There is this one cute guy who asked her to go to the social. His name is Craig, and she thinks he is the only one she really would like to escort her to the church social. Craig's grandparents attend the church, but not his parents; Lena doesn't think they come around the church at all. Well, she hasn't seen or heard of them since she came to this church. She once heard a rumor when one of the young ladies was talking, saying that she heard his father didn't want him, but Lena is not one to pay attention to rumors. She thinks everyone deserves a chance; didn't she get one? She does notice a lot of the young ladies go for Craig, and wonders why? Yes, he's cute and all, but the other guys are, too, in their own way.

Then she starts to wonder why he picked her when he could take his pick of any girl he wants. And she would be glad to be seen with him. They say he has a good job as a paralegal, and he's in law school, and one day he is going to be a great lawyer. Yet she also hears that some of the mothers of these young ladies do not want Craig dating their daughters. Some just say they don't want their daughters dating and in serious relationships. But they don't know their daughters are sneaking out on Saturday evenings to this little soda shop on the strip where Lena used to work. She saw some of them back in the old days, just didn't know they went to church and all. Well, she guesses it doesn't do any harm to socialize a little bit, not a lot, she just doesn't want to get hurt. Besides, everyone is getting ready for the church social and to go back to school, and the summer break is quickly coming to an end.

Lena has been hard at work studying and finishing up her GED, so she will be able to go to the local college this fall. If it hadn't been for all the help and encouragement of Mother Burns, and other helpful people who were determined to see her make it, she didn't think she would ever have her GED. And even more, she certainly would not be preparing to go to college this fall. Mother Burns has taught her to cook and clean properly. And how to keep herself a chaste young woman until the day she gets married. Sometimes she fantasizes about being married and in love and the person being in love with her for who she is.

Lena is moving into her own apartment next week; Mother Burns has been helping her gather up some things for it. She's so excited; it is a one-bedroom and so much better than the old place she lived in before. The hallways are so much brighter and cleaner. She is going to enjoy being on her own this time around, and her future looks brighter to her now. She did well on her GED, and now the counselor said she did great on her entrance exams for college as well. The counselor also told her that she has been accepted for the fall semester. It has been hard, but she has been studying all her free time, and some of her sleep time, too. But, not to let Mother Burns see; she says we must all get our proper rest in order to function at our very best. She says it helps a person to think, and it helps a person to grow and, it helps to, well, just plain old feel good every morning at the start of the day. Lena studies her Bible, and all the books about education that she can get her hands on. She wants to become a social worker, so she can help other people who are out there like she was, to give them some help and a chance like she got.

Now it is time to get ready for the church social. It's only a few days away, and Lena doesn't even have a dress for it. Mother Burns assures her all is well, and she would go shopping with Lena. She still hasn't accepted a date yet; maybe everyone has decided upon their dates. She felt it was already too late to pick the one whom she wants to take her to the social.

Tonight is the church social. They did find her a nice dress to wear, and she feels very pretty in it. Mother Burns and some of the other mothers of the church did all the cooking, and it looks and smells great. Everyone looks so nice and they are being so polite to each other. Wow, most of the young men and young ladies come in groups and not as couples. There is a lot of nice music playing, and Lena watches the guys and young ladies dance, who want to dance. Lena, on other hand, decides to help serve the food, and she smiles a lot when the young men say she looks nice. They keep asking her to dance, but she says no and thanks them for asking. Well, that was up until Craig came to the serving table. He starts making a lot of funny sad faces, telling her he would be making them all night until she dances with him. He is kind of cute, so she dances with him. They laugh a lot and have some punch and cookies, no real food, because they are talking and laughing too much. After the social is over, he asks for her phone number; she tells him that she doesn't have one, so he gives her his number.

A week or so after the church social, Craig asks Lena out on a date. He knows Mother Burns, so after Sunday morning service, he asks her also if it would be all right to take Lena to the movies and an early dinner. She tells Craig to bring her back early, so he promises that he will. And that's the day they go out on their first date. Lena and Mother Burns had made a pact that no one was to know that Lena lives alone; they are to think that she lives with Mother Burns. So after Craig drops her off at Mother Burns' house, she, in turn, drives Lena to her apartment, and in the event that he calls, she will give Lena the message the next day. Mother Burns would always say to be careful, and, "Keep yourself in a Godly manner, and when the time is right and you marry, God will honor and bless you in it."

After a while, Craig gets tired of calling and always having Mother Burns say that Lena is busy or not available. So he starts pressuring her, and she tells him where she works. Then he starts to meet her there after she gets off work in the late afternoon. She would go right to work, ever since she started classes this fall at the junior college. Now Craig is there whenever she gets off, and he is always kissing and hugging on her a lot. A lot more than she thinks she is ready for at the time. One evening, after one of their many dates, he drops her off at Mother Burns' house, and as always, she drives Lena to her place. But tonight, Craig calls Mother Burns, and by then she is in a deep sleep, so before she can think, she tells him that Lena is at home. Lena felt that this might happen because he has kept her out later than usual, hugging and kissing, and every time she tries to stop him, he keeps saying just one more, over and over again. She knows it is a mistake because she can see that they are both getting all hot and bothered. So she asks him to drop her off at Mother Burns', which he has been doing all the time they have been dating. She knows it is late, and Mother Burns would be tired, seeing it is past her bedtime. But Lena knows Mother Burns doesn't want Craig to know where Lena lives for real. She knows he will call back, but she just has to take that chance, and maybe he might feel it is too late to be calling Mother Burns. Besides, she has to go home and work on her homework, seeing as she hasn't finished it.

The very next day, Craig shows up at her job, not with gifts or flowers but asking her where she really lives and says if she feels anything for him and trusts him, she will tell him the real truth. He then starts saying, "I thought you lived with Mother Burns. How many other secrets have you been keeping from me? I thought we were a couple? Don't you love me or feel anything toward me?" So Lena breaks down and tells him where she lives, but makes him swear not to tell anyone else about it; he promises, and she believes him.

So they start to go out on dates without Mother Burns' knowledge, and back to Lena's place, always a lot of hugging, kissing, and touching now.

Now Craig has begun to press her harder to become intimate. She has held him off as long as she could. She keeps telling Craig that she wants to be married when she takes this step, and she is saving herself for that very reason. She knows she should talk to Mother Burns, but didn't want her to know Lena had broken 'their' promise, so she keeps it to herself. She should have talked to someone and gotten some advice on how to handle this situation, but she keeps listening to Craig, and what he wants, always in her ear, telling her that he loves her.

And when that doesn't work, Craig begins telling her how much he needs her and how she really needs him, too. And if she really loves him, like she says she does, then she will show him. Lena admits to herself that she is falling hard for Craig and she doesn't want to lose him.

So one Saturday after Christmas, Craig comes over to Lena's place. The one day when she can't take the pressure anymore, after Craig gets her where she becomes so hot and bothered, she just gives in to her feelings and desires for him. She wants it, but on the other hand, she is afraid, and she knows this will hurt GOD. But how can she lose Craig, especially when he is always telling her how much he loves her? And to please let him show her just how much he loves her. She asks herself, *Is this love or not?* Then, Craig begins kissing her again, and she just stops thinking altogether. She just wants to be there with him.

After the first time, they are intimate most of the time when they are together. Sometimes now, it seems they never go out anymore; all Craig wants is to get busy all the time. They hardly ever talk anymore; they used to laugh, talk for hours on end, and always go out to a show and to dinner at different restaurants. Now, they just order in from some take-out place close by. He tells her, "The faster we eat and the less talking we do, the more time we'll have to get busy." She still wants to talk to him about her day at work and at school.

One day, Craig tells her to stop all the talking. "Let's get busy; you know this is why I'm here, right?" At that moment, she feels like she is back in the old days, on the streets, listening to one of the many 'Johns.' "So, Lena, what's it going to be? Are you going to do a lot of talking tonight? Then if that's the case, I will just have to leave and go somewhere else where I don't have to hear a lot of yakking."

After each time, Lena repents and tells God how sorry she is, but that she has come to depend on Craig. Now, more times than not, she feels the old days are here again. Only, she's in love and doesn't want to lose him. *He promised to marry me once or twice, but now I'm not even sure he even likes me or sees me as a person. He no longer wants to know how my day was, and I don't think he even cares anymore. Did he ever?* Those are the questions she keeps asking herself. He used to bring flowers and gifts; now it's all about getting busy. Another evening when Craig came over and she asked him a question, he shouted at her, "If this is how it is going to be tonight, then I'm leaving right now!" so he just left.

Craig hasn't been coming around much lately; he says he hasn't been in the mood to be with her. She calls him on the phone, begging and pleading with him to stay with her, and she will do whatever he wants to do, "Just don't leave me." Now, when she calls him at work or home, he says he is busy, or he doesn't answer, and if he does, he says he will call back later, which he never does. Now Craig doesn't even come over, not even to get 'busy,' as he's always saying; these days, Lena just cries a lot. She talks to GOD even less; she knows that HE has to be very disappointed in her, because she is. Sometimes, she even gets mad at GOD because HE shouldn't have let this happen to her.

She hasn't been to church in a while; she tells Mother Burns she has a lot of studying to do to keep up with her grades. Lena knows it's a lie, but Mother Burns is always telling her that she's praying for Lena. She tells Mother Burns a little about her and Craig, and that they had broken up. She doesn't tell her that Craig has broken her heart and spirit. When she does go to church, Craig is now up behind this young lady named Susan. Mother Burns had asked Craig about Lena, but he told her she didn't want to go out anymore with him, and he just wanted to have fun.

Now, when Lena does go to church, her head is down, and she doesn't lift her hands high anymore to praise GOD. She just says, "GOD knows all about me, and HE understands me. How could I be so dumb? Craig said he loved me, he even held me like he did. So how did he fall out of being in love with me so quickly? Wasn't I pretty enough for him? Didn't I give him everything he asked of me; wasn't it enough for him? Or was I just a fool with blinders on?"

Well, some time has passed, and now Lena has started to turn to the LORD for HIS help. She tells HIM, "GOD, you have a lot of work to do on and in my heart." Then she tells HIM she needs so much help. She's made so many mistakes, and she asks HIM, can HE ever forgive her for turning away from HIM?

It is summer break again. She sees Craig at church when he comes, and he doesn't even look in her direction. But it's okay, because she knows GOD is loving her these days more and more. As she draws closer to HIM in reading her Bible and praying, HE draws closer to her. All she had to do was repent and turn away from her ways and run to HIM, and HE will help her through any and everything that comes her way. Now she has learned that HE is a faithful GOD, and most of all, HE forgives her!

Chapter Two

Craig

*Craig is a fictionalized character who deals with his rejection in
the form of lust, be it with money or with the flesh (in his body).*

Craig had been raised by his loving grandparents, Deacon Henry
and Mother Bessie Towers. The Towers were well respected in the
community as well as in the church.

Craig came to live with the Towers just a little after his third birthday.
He enjoyed being with his grandparents because they always made him feel
special. He knew that they loved him, but sometimes he wondered why he
no longer lived with his mom and dad. He tried to remember if he had done
something wrong. One day, Craig tried asking his grandfather as to why he
lived with them instead of being back at home with his own parents. His
grandfather's response was, "Me and your grandmother have a whole lot of
love to give, so we decided to give it to you." That was okay at first, but as
Craig got older, he needed and wanted to know more. He wondered why he
only saw his mother but not his father. He was always told that he worked a
lot and that he was busy but that his dad loved him very much.

Until one day, the truth came out when Craig was about eleven, as it
always does. Everyone knows a lie can only go on for so long. After he and
his cousin Derrick had played for a long while, Craig began to get tired
of playing, so he asked Derrick for his game back. But Derrick wanted
to continue playing, and after asking for his game numerous times, Craig
decided to snatch the game out of Derrick's hands. This made Derrick
angry. He was being selfish and spoiled as usual; he had gotten mad with
Craig for taking the game from him. In his anger, he screamed at Craig,
"That's why your daddy didn't want you and made your momma give you
away." Craig was so upset, feeling he had been lied to by everyone, he just
started hitting Derrick so many times with his fist. Their grandmother
heard the commotion and came upstairs to see what was going on. When
she got to Craig's room, Craig was out of control, beating up on Derrick.
Their grandmother screamed for them to stop fighting, and they did, but by
the time she stopped the fight, Craig had bloodied Derrick's nose and
blackened his right eye. His grandmother was so upset that she whipped

Craig for the first time ever since he'd been with them. His grandmother usually would talk to him, but not this time.

Later that evening, after his grandfather came home, his grandparents sat Craig down for a serious talking. They explained that what Derrick had said was the truth, but they didn't want him to find out that way. Craig's grandparents said that they wanted to tell him when they felt the time was right. Really, when is it ever the right time to tell anyone that they weren't wanted, especially by their own parents? His grandparents explained that his dad wasn't his dad, but that his mom had become lonely and ended up having a brief affair, and that she was sorry for what she had done. And since his dad couldn't handle taking care of some other man's baby, they sent Craig here to live with his grandparents. So Craig asked them, "What about my real dad? Why hasn't he come to visit me?" They told him that his real dad was a postman, and never knew about him. With his limited understanding of what happened, Craig had a very hard time dealing with knowing that the only father he knew had rejected him. Not for what he did, but for what his mother had done. Now he kind of understood why only his mother came for visits, not him.

That was when Craig began to build up a hate inside for his mother, for what she had done to him. That was what opened the door of 'hurt;' then the enemy was able to enter into Craig's young mind and heart. Now Craig also hated his dad for not wanting him, no matter what the reason was. "If they are my parents, aren't they supposed to love me?" Wasn't he entitled to have a father who loved him, one like his cousin has? Yes, his grandparents loved him, but all his buddies had a mom and dad. Now, Craig began to realize that he didn't really have either of his parents.

After some time had passed, Craig started asking his mom a lot of questions about why and how could she do this to him? From that time on, his mother didn't come around as much as she usually did. She still made sure that she brought him clothes, gifts, and money. But if she sensed that Craig was around, she'd leave in a hurry, trying to make sure that he didn't see her. His mother, because he now reminded her of her guilt and shame, didn't let Craig to get even a glimpse of her. Unfortunately for Craig, now he only saw his mother twice a year, on his birthday and Christmas. She rarely talked to him anymore, for fear of more unwanted questions and more blame. Now his mom was missing in action more than she ever was before. Craig's mom arrived late to his eighth-grade graduation, and she didn't even bother to show up at his high-school graduation at all. Craig had done very well in high school; he graduated with honors, and he received a full scholarship to go to college.

After Craig went to college, he wanted some extra money, so he applied at a prestigious law firm. He got the job. He had various duties to perform but his main job came later. Any time his boss had to go out of town on business, Craig was responsible for making all the reservations. His boss didn't want his secretary handling them any longer; he said it took a man to know what a man really likes. His grandfather was so proud of him, that he told Craig that he was the son that he had always wanted. Somehow or another, there was still a void in Craig's life, left there by his parents. His grandmother was always telling him how much GOD loved him and always taking him to church. His grandmother has been reading and teaching him the Bible since he was three. Yet Craig had always felt unloved by everyone, even GOD.

Craig has grown into a very handsome young man, and he has learned to use it to his advantage, yet he is one who deals with a lot of secrets. Craig now lives away at school on campus, where he still gets good grades, and on the surface, he seems to be very successful. Somehow, he hasn't realized that he has failed in the most important area of his life. He doesn't even think about reading his Bible or praying. He feels that GOD has let him down. We must understand that there is no failure in God, but it is failure in man. So all his grandparents' teaching and training on the WORD of GOD just goes out the window while he is away at school. He only picks up a Bible when he comes home on breaks, to keep up appearances. Craig has never dealt with the real issues in his heart, so now he wants someone, anyone else to pay for what happened to him. Craig feels that everyone, even GOD let him down a long time ago, and now satan is using Craig's hurt to his advantage. With the help of satan, Craig has now become the perpetrator. So rather than getting the necessary help and dealing with the emotions that come when one feels alone, hurt, and rejected, Craig now has two different personalities. He plays quiet around the church and at the job. But at school, especially on the weekends, he's known as the man about town. Craig has become well known for breaking one girl's heart after another.

He seems to have forgotten all about how much GOD loves all of HIS creations, especially people. Craig forgot the commandment to love thy neighbor as yourself. However, he cannot, because he doesn't love himself. Craig is so messed up on the inside, now he can't help even himself to stop the thing that he has given his 'will' over to, that is, something that Craig has allowed to dwell on the inside of himself. Now Craig's campus lifestyle is following him into the church. Craig has set his sights on a young lady at his church named Lena. Craig became interested in her when he came home on one of his school breaks. He has never really talked to Lena or met her. He is just so curious about her. Craig has just been asking around about her, only to find out very little about Lena through the church grapevine, the younger gossipers, some of his peers. With not much to go on, it was all Craig needed, just enough to wet his appetite and strike up his curiosity and interest even more. He felt it would take a little while, but he knew if he acted, walked, and talked like he was saved, he would score. Craig had to play the game so he could get Lena interested in him. Craig never feared he wouldn't get her; he just knew he would. Or his name wasn't Craig the Crab Conqueror, the one who could pull any girl down, that is, to the bottom of the bed.

Craig never takes a second thought that Lena is GOD's child, but him being in a backsliding state and blinded by the enemy of his soul, he doesn't care to look. What happened to Galatians 6:7-10? "Be not deceived; God is not mocked: for whatsoever a man soweth, that shall he also reap. For he that soweth to his flesh shall of the flesh reap corruption; but he that soweth to the Spirit shall of the Spirit reap life everlasting. And let us not be weary in well doing: for in due season we shall reap, if we faint not. As we have therefore opportunity, let us do good unto all men, especially unto them who are of the household of faith." His grandmother taught it to him over the years. He just wants to hurt someone because he is hurting. Craig knows that two wrongs don't make a right.

Craig always began by putting on his quiet charm and his smooth speech, not too heavy and not too fast. However devastating as it may be, this is his MO. So unfortunately, by the time Craig was finished with a young woman, she did not know what had hit her. His hope for them, for all the females, is that once he is done with her, that she will be under so much rubble that she won't know which way is up, much less know what happened or how she got there. His plan is that she will be so embarrassed by the experience that she won't tell a soul about it. Isn't Craig just like satan, who comes to kill, steal, and destroy you? Craig was taught that satan, as well as GOD, needs people to do his bidding in this Earthly realm. Now we see that Craig is willfully carrying out the intents of satan, who is the enemy of everyone's soul. Craig likes to play his game with the girls, then before they know it, Craig goes in for the kill, well, the spoils anyway. Like it or not, Craig is determined to deflower them, love them, and then leave them, in love and completely lost. There is a story going around the school about the first year Craig arrived on campus. The story goes something like this: they tell of a girl who went home on the Christmas break and killed herself over Craig. Maybe someone should have told her about CHRIST and HIS undying love and HIS mercy and grace. GOD would have forgiven her no matter what; all, she had to do was ask HIM.

It is late, and Craig is at home, doing a lot of thinking about how to divide and conquer. *Well,* Craig says, *Lena is sort of a challenge for me. She has that Mother Burns always hanging around.* Craig is now beginning to devise a way around this present situation. After studying Lena for a while, Craig finds his answer. See, once Craig finds out that Lena has her own place, Craig knows he was home free. "All I have to do is to get Lena to fall in love with me, tell her that I love her a couple of times, and she will become putty in my hands." See how Craig is now telling lies like his father, satan? "I can now mold and shape Lena my way, to my likings, and when I am finished, I'll just discard her like the clay she is. You know all girls are like clay, they need to be molded." Craig has forgotten that they only need to be molded by the love of GOD. "Females need direction, they want to be told this and shown that, and what to say and how to do it. Lena isn't my first and she won't be my last to conquer. I am telling you the truth; I feel so good when I get what I want, and I never really care about them. I only care about myself and what I want. Isn't that what both my dads did to my mom and me, then my mom did it to me? My thing is, one turn deserves another and another until we all die." Doesn't the Bible say that we should forgive one another of our trespasses (Matt. 6:14)? The real deal behind Craig is that he feels that women are weak, so he preys on their weakness. In his heart, Craig feels that is what men have been doing since the world has been in existence.

"You see, I go to the nightclubs just to meet all kinds of women, especially the married ones. Yes, I've had a few married women too. What's wrong with that? Weren't my mother and my father both married to other people? You see, I found out my real dad was separated from his wife when he and my mom got involved. Well, that's water under the bridge, and no one cries over spilled milk, especially not me. I have shed my tears, and now I make others cry (1 Cor. 5:10). You know that some married women are just like me, broken and filled with desires and looking for a way to fill the void in their lives.

"They want more and more, and to be told that they are pretty and that you love them.

"That's how I got my first car, from this forty-something old broad. She had money, the kind I really like; she kept spending her husband's money on me, and besides, he was always away. So I became her distraction. She wanted to try to relive her youth through and with me. She would shop for me and buy me expensive gifts to keep me interested. Therefore, when she thought I was getting bored, she paid cash to get me a car. The relationship only lasted few weeks; about the time hubby found out, that was when all the bank statements and credit cards bills came in. But, as for me, by that time, I was already on the move and in flight to my next prey as fast as I could and especially now that I had new wheels. Wildly, I was off to greener pastures to see who or what I could devour today. See, I was getting busy with her best friend, also. While they were competing with each other for my attention, all I really wanted was the money. I never admitted to either of them that I was seeing the other one. They were at each other's throats already; they didn't need my interference. I used to hear them on the phone while on a date with the other one. Maybe that was just the 'cats' showing each other their claws. I made sure that I never went to the same places that I took the other woman. If one of them asked to go to a place I had been, I would always throw a wrench into the situation and ask them, what if someone sees us together, how would you explain it?

"After some time had passed, I began to keep a little black notebook to help me keep all appointments and women straight. When I really got the hang of it, I started to play the game even harder and stronger. My motto is: Love them, leave them, but get all you can, and make sure that you are satisfied with the prey that you have conquered. Then you can move on to the next one with no regrets.

"At my present job, the boss's wife has been making eyes at me, but you know me, I must remain shy and quiet. I mustn't reveal my 'true' self. She is always giving me a lot of those so-called light compliments about my bluish-green eyes, and says my curly hair is always so neat. One day, she slipped her number into my shirt pocket when she felt no one was looking. However, I will never call her; I'm waiting for her to make her move. She finally did; one Friday, when I left work, she was in the parking lot standing near my car. I thought a lot to myself, seeing that she's got it really bad, and now I'm going to see just how bad she really has it. Understand, my job is solely to benefit me. Now I have to get her to pay for what she wants and for what she is seeking. Then she has to pay me a lot for her bad behavior. I often talk to myself, saying, 'Be cool, Craig, this is a big cat, we must see if she is really willing to pay for a little adventure."

That evening after work, when Craig sees her pacing back and forth outside near his car, he walks to his car acting like he isn't paying attention to her. Craig gets into his car, and drives out of the lot, just slow enough for her to keep up and follow him to the place that he is leading her to. *So what of it? She took the bait.* She follows Craig all the way to the little restaurant right off the highway. He picks a booth all the way in the back and orders a large Coke. Now, once again he's telling himself to be patient and know that it will pay off. Here goes, she comes in, and she's looking around, seeing if she can spot him, but in the meantime, she orders a Coke and asks if they have a ladies' room. *Ladies' room, yeah, right in this dinky joint, she just needed an excuse to walk farther into the place.* Oh, she found him all right;

now she gives him a cockamamie story. Something that she just made up to try and trick him into getting what she really wants. It is all a made-up lie, that story about how she's gotten lost. And how she was about to ask for directions after she had used the ladies' room, but since she spotted Craig in the booth, just maybe he could help her. And while she is telling Craig this, she is sliding her butt down in the booth. Not knowing that she is the one who is being hunted all the time. Therefore, Craig continues to play shy, leaving her up to playing her little tricks. No sooner does she sit down than she starts playing her games with him.

That is why he chose the last booth in the back; Craig knows her type. Her kind always does that. Craig has studied and surveyed all types of women, especially her type, and they are all the same. First, she starts by touching his hair, saying that she always wanted to know how it felt. Women love to touch Craig's hair, and they say that he has nice, soft, dark curly hair. They tend not to be able to restrain themselves from touching it. It just seems to drive them crazy once they touch it. He just has not found out why yet, but he uses it to his advantage. So let them touch it, go right ahead, they will pay for that too in the long run, no matter how short of a run it may be. She starts asking him questions about his job and did he like working there. Then she gives him that sheepish grin while she goes into her act. Craig knows all along how the game is played so he looks up slightly, as if he isn't even interested. All the while, he's sizing her up and counting up his dollars in his head at the same time. All the while, she is trying hard to keep his attention. He knows that she is about to have a meltdown, so he informs her that it's time for him to leave.

Then he leads her to his next destination, which is a nightclub that he chose in advance. No doubt this is one of the clubs where he has taken some of his other prey. After only a few drinks, she is all over Craig, and it is now time for him to leave once again. She proceeds to follow him outside, and he pretends to help her get into her car, and all the while he's helping her, Craig is accidently rubbing up against her lightly, but just enough that she notices. She's a little drunk, but she's not stupid; now she starts pulling at him and trying to grab hold of anything to get a kiss. So he kisses her and then pulls away very quickly. Now it is time for Craig to be headed home, but not before he gives her his number so that she could make her next move. See, it is Friday, and old hubby isn't due back until Monday night late; remember, Craig is the person in charge of making old hubby's reservations.

"It's Saturday morning, and I'm trying to get some rest. But she has already started calling me early today, on a false pretense that her husband needs something at the office. She wants me to meet her at 6:00 p.m. at the job so that she will be able to fax the papers right to him. While reminding me of his many meetings that 'hubby' will be in and out of all that day, she told me that she needed me because she does not know her way around the office that well. Furthermore, she does not even work there, and she does not want to mess up the files. Now, all kinds of thoughts are going through my head. Why at 6:00 p.m.? I know that everyone leaves the office around two o'clock on Saturdays, and a few stragglers leave between two-thirty and three o'clock. However, that is not the case today; since the boss is away, everyone will leave early, and I do mean everyone. Why? She wants to get busy with me of course, and also to make sure that there is no one else in the building. The only way to get in the building after six in the evening is to enter through the back door right off the parking lot, and the only elevator that is running is the back elevator, how convenient is that?

"It was 6:00 p.m. sharp when I drove up on the lot. I looked around to see if anyone else was there, and to see if I could spot her. Upon entering the building, I didn't see her either, but as soon as the elevator door opened, she hopped right inside it. I asked her where she just popped out from; she just laughed as the elevator doors closed. Once on the elevator, I pushed the button for the 22nd floor, and as soon as the elevator started up, she opened up her coat to let me see that she was wearing a low-cut, see-through blouse. I didn't dare react; I just acted as if I wasn't paying any attention to her. The elevator came to a stop on our floor, the door opened, and we both stepped off at the same time. While we walked down the hallway to the corner office to my boss's office, she was just yapping away. Then she told me that my boss told her just where the files were, and wouldn't you know they would be in the section of his office where we couldn't be spotted even if someone did come up to the office? Then she gave me instructions to turn on the lights and go into his closet to get the files that were conveniently supposed to be on the top shelf and that besides, she'd been unable to reach them.

"Well, at this point in the game, I knew that she was lying, but I went along with her, playing the dumb row with the nice little wife. After looking for the files only a few moments, just to give her time to do what she did, I began asking her was she sure that he said in his personal closet? She kept instructing me to look all the way on the very top shelf. I kept telling her that I couldn't find the files, and did my boss mention to her exactly where it was on the top shelf, because he had a lot of boxes marked 'personal' up there? Then, no sooner than that, I asked her did he mention to her that it could possibly be in the file cabinet if we couldn't find it in the closet? Hastily, she plays her hand, before I can come down and out of the closet, she ran in, prepared to get all that she has planned for, the very reason we were there for real in the first place. Once again she started the rubbing game, first my head, and then my arms, talking about how strong they felt. I pretended again to resist. She started kissing on me and removing my sweater, which I willingly let her do, playing along with her. Remember, she thought and felt that she was in control. I asked her, what if someone were to walk in here right now, what would they think, how would this look to them, how would we explain this? She then told me that no one is ever in the building at this time on a Saturday evening.

"This told me one thing: that she has done this before. Should I dare wonder how many times and how many guys has it been? I wondered if maybe she caught hubby there with his date and it was payback time. Well, it really didn't matter to me; I was just there for the money. She just didn't know it yet. I began to wonder whether or not she was just a lonely lady. Now, don't get me wrong, I came for the same reason that she came for, only I wanted to be paid for my troubles; besides, she was a good-looking lady. Anyway, she came looking for me, not the other way around. Why? Because she thinks I'm shy and quiet and that I won't say anything, and for what, so that I can lose my great-paying job? So we started getting busy, and then we were done and I'm sure that I have conquered my prey. If she requires more, she will have to pay for it, and pay dearly she must.

"Afterward, while we were leaving the office, I reminded her of the files and that we mustn't forget them, letting her think that I thought that was the only reason we really came there in the first place—or did we? She then informed me that her hubby will have to get them on Monday when he returns. As I punched for the elevator, she tried to kiss me goodnight, but the elevators doors opened right away. Remember, we were the only ones in the building. As we ride down, I began to ask her a lot of questions about herself. While she was trying to answer the first one, I asked her another one, right after the one I just asked. Wow, I thank my lucky stars the elevator doors open, and I rushed out the door, telling her I'm tired. She ran right outside behind me, and I drove off, leaving her in the parking lot, while telling myself, 'Boy, you are good, just be patient a little longer, payday is only a few hours away.'"

The next day, she starts calling, real early on a Sunday. Craig has started thinking to himself, *Does she ever rest?* He could just beat her; it's only six in the morning. *I am not going to answer my phone this early unless it is a fire, but knowing her, it is a fire—one of her own doing.* He lets her leave a message, to answer her later on when he decides to get up. Boy, what's the real emergency? Now she is calling every fifteen minutes, and it is only just little past 7:00 a.m. *I know this broad is tripping, but that only means I did one darn heck of a job on her. I should give myself a pat on the back; well, what did I expect?*

Now he's thinking, *Here comes my pay, and it is hot and burning in her purse.* Smiling, he says, "Payday, here I come," as he lies back down to rest just a bit more. He doesn't answer her until around 8:30 a.m.; now she seems kind of steamed when he finally answers his phone. He told her he was asleep and that he would get back with her later. Well, he knows she's mad, but this is his game, and he make the rules. At about 10:00 a.m., his door buzzer starts buzzing. He goes over and sees who it is, and it's her, of course. So he buzzes her in. Wow, she is very resourceful; she went into the files at the job to find out where he lived. *This will be another charge for her,* he thinks, while waiting for her in his doorway. He asks her what is wrong. She has yet another lie on her tongue; she tells him that her husband, Craig's boss, called her at 7:00 a.m. for the file or some contents that are in them. *What, now she thinks I'm stupid? She started calling me at 6:00 a.m.* He asks her how she knew where he lives, and she tells the first truth in days. She says that she went to the office and looked in his employee file. After that, she starts lying to him again, saying she only did it because she needed his help. *Yeah, she wants me and her to get busy again, or maybe she is just not dealing with a full deck from jump.* Why couldn't she just get the file that hubby needed while she was in the office getting *his* file? That's because she has got it bad, and he is about to find out really how bad does she have it. So she asks, can she sit down. Craig says yes. He'll play along with her. Before she sits down, she takes off her coat to show off her clothing. She's looking a bit hungry, trying not to seem starved. But he knows that look, and he knows that she really is hungry; he's no fool. *Now, how much will she be willing to pay for another encounter?* he thinks as he sits down on the couch across from her. Then he asks her point blank, "What are you really here for? And what do you really want from me?" He tells her they can't repeat last night, and that he could get fired if anyone found out, then how would he pay his bills, and how and where would he get another job? He just starts shooting all these questions at her to see what she will say and what she is willing to do. Then she says, "I've got money, money of my own," so he tells her that he can't take her money. Of course, her words are music to his ears. Now she says, "How much will you need?" while she is reaching for her checkbook. Then he tells her once again that he can't take her money. In the back of his mind, he's saying, *Yes, I can, and, yes, I will take your money.* Then she asks, "Will 5 Gs be enough to cover your expenses?" By this time, she has started filling out the check. Then, when he feels she is almost finished writing, he says to her, "I only take cash, but that I will hold on to it until you can exchange it for the cash."

Now for the first time, she begins to realize that she is the prey and not the hunter, and that all the time, she was really the one who was being played and hunted. Then she starts calling Craig names that his mother hadn't named him, so he told her that she could leave now with no strings attached and that nothing more will be said on the matter.

But if she decides to stay, then she would be required to pay for what she wants. So she hurries up and writes the check and gives it to Craig. He checks the spelling and makes sure it is signed properly, then takes it and locks it in his bedroom for safekeeping, all the while telling her to stay put, and that he will deal with the particulars in a few moments.

On the way back, his phone starts ringing, so he answers it. Who could guess who it is? It is Craig's boss, telling him that he got finished with his meetings early, and could Craig please pick him up at the airport in the morning, about five o'clock. He says he wants to surprise his wife and spend the whole day with her, so Craig tells him it is not a problem and that he will see him soon and hangs up the phone. Then he drops the bomb on her, telling her the good news that hubby will be coming home earlier than he was expected. So now he tells her that he is no longer in the mood and that he has some things to take care of before getting up at 4:00 a.m. to pick up the husband. But this is to get out of kissing her. So now they go through the same routine as yesterday, and after they're finished, she just can't wait; she wants to know when she will get to see him again. His answer to her is the same as to all the married ones: when they get the money and only when hubby leaves town again. She leaves angry but very satisfied. So now he has hooked yet another bank account; besides, she is really a bonus.

"Back to my dear Lena; she played hard, I told her what she wanted to hear and needed to hear. But what I needed was to get what I wanted, to divide and conquer; see, it is the satisfaction of knowing that I have conquered, that is the highlight of my day, and besides, that is what the game is all about, right?

"Now, where are we? Ah, yes, I have to make sure that they don't tell anyone about me or what they did with me. Lena wanted me bad, and she didn't want me to leave her, so she did everything that I asked of her. She got busy with me as much as I wanted and as often as I wanted until I found another prey that I just had to have and conquer. Lena, she fell very hard for me, always talking and talking until I didn't even want her anymore. She really was good, kind of experienced, I sometimes felt, but that's all over for me, I have moved on to greener pastures. Lena, she just can't let go, it's over, but she keeps calling all times of day and night. What up with that? Doesn't she know when to call it quits? Go on back to the church and to her GOD, HE will forgive her, but me, I've got to get Susan in the sack."

Chapter Three

Susan

Susan is a fictionalized character; she has turned the tables and has become the perpetrator herself.

I come from a long line of rejection, and if Craig thinks that he is going to do me like he did Lena, he is sadly mistaken. I heard how she was so stupidly into Craig and how he's been hinting to the guys at church that another one bites the dust. Besides, he has gotten himself a real big problem

—*me*. See, I am a rejector, and proud of it. Yes, I will eat you up and spit you out. Once I'm finished with you, you'll look and feel like Swiss cheese. Don't get me wrong, I believe in GOD, and I give HIM what is HIS and/or what is due HIM. Oh yes, I pray to HIM every day; the only thing I ask HIM is for my health and strength, and I will do all the rest. HE has been faithful and dependable to me thus far, so I will continue to acknowledge HIM.

When I was young, I was beaten and treated very badly all of the time by my mom. Yes, by my very own mom, but she couldn't help herself; she was treated the same way. So was my grandmother, and others before them; since they weren't loved, they didn't show love, especially since no one really knew what the term 'love' meant or how it was to treat someone with love. They went with men who gave them a little money and, in turn, used them for a punching bag, then had sex afterward with them, all this just to say they got a man. Yeah, right, they have a man all right, the very scum of the earth, something that I now scrap off the bottom of my shoe. Never to be respected by him, or liked, and definitely not loved. They have now passed it on down from one generation to the next. Some even have had abortions or been made to have them. Beaten and broken, they have survived another messed-up generation.

I tried to be friends with other women, but they always wanted something or other from me. I was taught by them, and made to learn the ropes, whether I liked it or not, by them at very tender and early stage in life. That the only reason they would befriend me was that I had something that they wanted or were in need of. What they really wanted was, my man, his money, my crib, my life. I wasn't about all of that and besides, after that one time, a really bad and sad breakup, I was through with that love bug thingy. He got her, and she got him, and I got the heck out of Dodge. I decide I could do good or bad by myself. I didn't need a female as a friend and I didn't want one, either. Besides, they were weak, sneaky, and underhanded anyway, and I had no need nor desire to be near or around a weakling. I was strong then, and I still am now. I decided that I had what men wanted and I decided how everything would go on for my life. I had to make my own destiny. Now, please do not get it twisted: I never asked anyone for pity, love, care, or anything. And I never plan on doing it, either. The reason that I ask for nothing is because in turn, I give nothing, I just take. I will survive, I can make it, and I *will* make it, no matter what it may cost you. So, Craig, bring on your best, I am called Susan with No Soul. Cold as an iceberg, yet cool as a cucumber. I seek out my prey, and I make them pay, never to rest another day. Understand, it will cost you dearly to be with me, and it will cost you to utter my very name. Take notice of my list of charges; I will not alter them for anyone, not even GOD.

1. **Fifty thousand for dinner.**

2. **Five thousand for a kiss on the cheek and move away quickly.**

3. **Two thousand to touch my hair once and not long, and no holding it, period.**

4. **Three thousand to be seen with me, and nothing more.**

5. **Six thousand to hold my hand a fleeting second, and no squeezing of it is allowed.**

Ten thousand to go to the movies or theater with you, and nothing more. First of all, let's set the record straight from the beginning: I am not gay, just because I don't have sex with men. They couldn't pay for it, even if I were to consider it! I take all my prey to the mall to buy my next outfit (complete with shoes, purse, and jewelry) and then off to the beauty salon (hair, feet, and nails). I must look good and desirable at all times. I will not even consider a prey that doesn't have great hygiene, pretty teeth, wears nice clothes, have a nice ride, and please do not forget the most important part, that he must have a big fat bank account! Yes, money is everything to me, so even if a man has all the rest going for him and no money, I will not look in his direction.

Second, let me let you in on a little big secret: the real truth of the matter is, if he's broke, I wouldn't notice him even if he was right in front of me. I can smell a broke man miles away, I don't care how he is flashing. You see, I do intense research on my prey, married or not. I am the one who decides if he can play in my game or not. People who do not have these qualities, I do not waste my time on them, nor do I have pity on them.

Now Craig, he is an exception to the rule. I'm doing this as a charity case for someone else who will remain nameless. They needed my expertise. And, from the very moment that I found out who the target was, I decided to help them with gladness and joy in my heart. Craig needed to see the error of his ways, if only for a little while, and I know just how to do that. He was like the men who had been bringing women of my family down for years. I was so excited to help my new clients at this time in their lives. Craig has hurt them and caused them tremendous pain. Now it's my job to take care of him and even out the scales of justice, rather, to cause them to weigh in my favor. I must hurt him and make him pay dearly with every cent that he has or can get. Then, without any hesitation, I will send him on his way, never to turn my way again. Remember, I'm well trained, a very good fighter, and I know how to choose and use all my weapons well.

My list of prey, married or not:

    *Doctors with private practices and hospitals, have cash.

    *CEOs, who own the company and have a big fat salary, have cash.

    *Lawyers with a prestigious law firm or a private practice, have cash.

    *Fortune 500 tops have lots of liquid cash.

    *Football players have lots of cash.

    *Baseball players have lots of cash.

    *Basketball players have lots of cash.

    *Pro golfers have lots of cash. I like my sports players to be kind of dumb, but not too dumb.

    My list of no-nos, no matter what:

    *Students most definitely are no-nos, period.

    *Bus drivers, train conductors, plane pilots, and truck drivers.

    *NO kids (whether or not they are kids of CEOs, doctors, lawyers, or anybody else's kids for that matter).

    *No pimps or drug dealers.

    *Bankers, even if he owns his own bank.

    *Junk men, I don't care if he owns a fleet of junkyards, I will not have him on any level.

    *Car dealers, owner or not.

Now if it's not on this list, it is not worth mentioning. I stand by the standards that I have set. I always get paid up front, at all times, with all expenses paid up front, also. Contracts must be signed and notarized so that the other parties have a crystal-clear understanding of what is expected of them and that there are no strings attached.

Back to our lover-boy Craig. He must pay; I have to get all his money and break him. I've allotted myself eighteen days or fewer, I believe; the fewer, the better. So here we are; Craig has set up a meeting to bring me 5 Gs in cash to be seen with me; my rule is, it must always be in cash. I brought along a couple of buddies, so that I won't have to break a nail. That in and of itself is another fee, and we really don't have the time to go into details about those arrangements. Craig arrives, I ask him for the money, he tries to touch my arm, but my guys grab him before he can. Craig has been instructed to hand me the money. I count it; it is all here. Then, I get up, and just walk away, leaving him at the table all by himself. Only so I can charge him twenty grand for our next encounter. Craig is left looking dumb and somewhat numb, but he's hooked, so I know he will be back. Then of course, I go and pay my guys for their time tonight. They really like payday any time of day or night.

Now Craig has already started calling my pay-per-minute cell phone early this morning. I don't feel like answering him right away; I just put the phone on vibrate and let him keep calling for a few more hours until I decide to answer, only to tell him it's off and then hang up. Most people would feel that they have been conned and walk away, but not Craig. He is really determined to get in touch with me; man, the boy must have my number on speed dial. Finally, I answer the phone, and he asking me what will it take to see me again? I tell him 20 Gs and no touching or my guys will not fail to put a hurting on him. Craig agrees and hangs up. I have given him all the details of when and where to meet me. I hope he will be able to follow all my instructions; for a little while there, he seemed not to understand what I was telling him. At first, he started to stutter, then he kept saying "huh" a lot, but the folks at church, they say he is very smart. You can't prove it by me. Craig called back later, to say he needed a few more days, but I told him that the clock was ticking and that he only had seven hours, or all bets were off.

Later on, me and the guys are chilling at the Highlander's Bar and Grill on the north side of town. While we are sitting down in the booth, laughing, one of my guys spots Craig; he's looking around the restaurant for me. So I tell my guy to go and bring our little purse, Craig, over to me. I have instructed the guys ahead of time that when he shows up, to go to the bar and get themselves a drink, since this will not take long at all. Now Craig has followed my guy to our booth. I told him to take a seat and I ask for the money, which he hands over with no problem. I then tell the guys to give us twenty minutes tops. The guys leave as I began to go into my routine of counting the 20 Gs. Craig blurts out, "Don't I get more than twenty minutes for my money?" as soon as I finish counting the cash; yes, it was all there. "I only conduct business after I'm paid in full," I tell him. All the time, Craig is watching my guys at the bar; now he asks me that same old lame question again, whining like "Don't I get more than twenty minutes for my money?" My answer to him is, "No." Then I get up to leave. I cannot stand spending one more minute with Craig; he asks too many questions and whines while asking them.

As I am getting up, I signal my guys that we are now finished and that they can escort Craig out of the restaurant like the punk he is. Now the guys return, and I ask them did they have any problems with Craig; see, I had informed my guys of the game plan earlier. To only roughen him up somewhat, but not to touch that handsome face, since I'm sure that is one of the ways he gets his money, the start, anyway. Now I figure that Craig is mad, but is he mad enough to give up? Especially since he feels that he can conquer me. That is so, so very sad on his part; the boy doesn't even realize that he is the one being conquered as we speak. Now look at him, my pay-per-minute phone is starting to ring again. Oh, I know it's Craig because this phone was bought for him and him only. I guess I should answer, since he has been calling now for about an hour or so. I answer and say, "Hello?" Then he blurts out, "This is me, Craig, I have 15 Gs, why don't we do dinner?" I say no, that is not what I charge for dinner. Then I tell him what my charge for dinner is. I call out his name, in my low sexy voice, saying, "Craig, it is going to cost you thirty, take it or leave it." He says okay, as I expect that he would. Then he nervously says he will need a few days to get the money. I told Craig that he only has until six o'clock tomorrow night. So I then give him instructions on where to meet me on tomorrow, at Fredda's Intimate Café at six o'clock, and not to be late or short. He says okay again, so I hang up the phone, and besides it's late, and I must get my beauty rest.

Good grief, I don't even feel like I have slept that long and Craig is already burning up my phone, what time is it anyway? I think, and at the same time look at my watch. It's not even ten yet, why is this boy burning up my phone so early? He has all of my instructions, doesn't he? I turn back over and decide to get a few more winks; at twelve, I decide to answer him. Now, before he can get hello out of his pretty little mouth, I informed him he has under a minute to speak because I am very busy, and time is money. He blurts out, "Hi, I've got the money," and that he will be at Fredda's at six. I hang up the phone, all the while laughing. I stop laughing somewhat, only to pick up the phone again to call my guys and tell them to get ready for another payday, or, pay night. We are now at Day Six, and I have to begin to up the prices, and I really don't have eighteen days to play around or waste on Craig. Even though when I took this job, I felt I could spare the time, the LORD knows I need and could use a vacation. Tonight, I will give him a kiss on the cheek and leave, seeing now I have to reel him in a lot faster than I had thought. Of course, we do not want the little fish to think about getting away and trying to escape my claws and net. We cannot have that, can we? See, Craig must pay, and he must pay dearly.

Okay, it is almost six, let's get the ball rolling, I don't have a lot of time tonight to hang out since my rest was broken so early today. We are at the table waiting on our little moneyman, Craig. He shows up on time, and the guys go to the bar for drinks and or maybe some girl company. Me, I start my count as soon as Craig hands over the money; ah, it's all here, all thirty grand. Now, Craig is ready to sit, eat, and talk, I tell him that I am not hungry, but I feel that I have a very expensive thirst coming on. Craig signals the waiter, then I order up a six-hundred-dollar bottle of wine. Craig pays for it, not with cash but with his American Express card. I think maybe he's broke already, so I pick up the bottle and lean over to give him a kiss on the cheek and leave. I bet Craig didn't see that coming. By the time he can try and make sense out of what just happened, my guys will be getting paid and we will be celebrating with his six-hundred-dollar bottle of wine.

Remember, I am 'Susan with No Soul.' Feelings are for the living; I died a long time ago. I am just getting paid for my troubles, past and present. Like it or not, I can only be found among the dead.

Now it's the next day, time for me to call the people who hired me for this job and give them some updates. I assured them that all was well and going along just as planned, and that I would be wrapping it up in a couple of days. They didn't sound happy or anything like that, just told me to finish the job as quickly as I could. I said okay and hung up. This really has to be over in a couple of days; see, I have a much larger fish to fry. Understand that this big fish is my own personal money for my pocket only. This thing with Craig is a charity case, and it has to be over quick, fast, and in a hurry. You don't think I would sacrifice my meal for him, do you? I never lose my money for anyone, especially not for the likes of Craig. With this case, I only receive a percentage, so, Craig, I am upping the stakes, do or die. I don't care if he cries; I just need to get paid, no matter what it will cost him. Now instead of Craig calling me, I will make the next move; besides, it's my game and I, and only I, make the rules, and only I can change them. I call Craig; I begin by telling him that we can be intimate if, and only if, he has 100 Gs. He is getting excited. I can hear it in his voice. He thinks that he is about to conquer me. I also inform him he only has two days to get the monies together and to meet me at the Browndale Hotel in the lobby at 8:00 p.m., and don't be late. I could hear him mourning when I was hanging up. I wonder about Craig, thinking that he might not have it, maybe he's already broke. Then I laugh. What a fool and what an idiot Craig is, that he would be willing to pay 100 Gs for sex. Well, he will recover once I am gone. He can revert back to his old ways and tricks. Craig knows one thing for sure: if he is short, that it is over, and I get to keep the money and then I can keep moving on to my next job, my next prey! I gave Craig two days; I figure that in two days he could do whatever he does to get the money that he needs. See, I heard, as I told you before, that he has a reputation. I will let him have his 'rep.' I just have to break him first. You think maybe he will wimp out, or try to be all that man he thinks he is?

Today is the day, and Craig hasn't called yet; guess you can say he bit off more than he could chew. You think he will be a no-show? He probably can't get half of it; that can mean only one thing to me: he's broke, and I can finally close this case out, my job here is done, and I can move on. The phone rings; who would have thought? It is Craig on the other end. I say hello, then he says hello, he's talking really fast, I can hardly understand him. "Are we still on for tonight?" I tell him yes, only if he can produce all the money that I had asked him for. He informs me that he will be a little late, only a few minutes. I tell him I will allow him to be fifteen minutes late, and only that.

We arrive at the hotel about ten to eight, and talk over the happenings of the evening, or in Craig's case, what may not be happening. While we are in the lobby having a few drinks and kicking it, lo and behold, about eight-fifteen, Craig comes rushing in so hard and fast he looks as if his eyes are going to pop out. He hurries up and hands me two envelopes. We sit down at the table. I go into my routine. Craig is sitting very quiet, and I start to count; the first envelope has 50 Gs, that's good. Now, when I began to pick up the second envelope, I notice Craig kind of sighs. I look up, because he now has my undivided attention. "Is this short, and if so, how much, and don't lie." Craig tells me it is about $150 short, so I go back to continue my count, and you know what? He was right, it is exactly $150 short. I begin to get up to leave. Craig asks, "Where is the room?" I tell him that there is no room, and that is because there isn't 100 Gs here. You were told 100 Gs or nothing, *correct*? I give him a hug, and he begins to cry, but by that time, I am gone for good. I toss that pay-per-minute phone in the trash; see, it was bought only to communicate with him.

Now I can say my job here is truly done. Believe me, I really do have a bigger fish to fry. As for the young lady who killed herself over Craig, this won't bring her back, but it might make him think about the next girl he hurts. See, before I gave him the hug, I slid her picture over to him. On the back of, it stated, "Although she is no longer with us, we still remember and love her. Now because of you she can only be found in a lonely cold grave."

Chapter Four

Alex

Alex is a fictionalized character who suffers from rejection because of the blindness of his good heart, and he is not able recognize this spirit of rejection when it shows up.

Alex is a good family man; he married his high-school sweetheart, Donna. Everything was all right in their world, and they had twin boys, two great kids, both in high school. Down through the years, Alex and Donna have had a few problems, but not enough for either of them to leave the marriage. Alex went to work in the evenings, but not before helping the boys with their homework assignments. He would always ask them about their day as he finished making their dinner. Alex wanted to make sure that they got at least one home-cooked meal each day.

Now that the twins have graduated from high school and have gone off to college, Alex has been feeling kind of lonely. His wife, Donna, is in school to get her Master's degree; she hadn't too long ago finished college and received her Bachelor's degree. Donna told Alex that it would be better if she just continued with her education while her brain was open to school, especially since her job was willing to pay for most of it, as long as she stayed with the company at least five years. They both had agreed that it was a good choice and move. Now that Donna is in school and working, she and Alex don't see each other that much, nor do they get to spend quality time together anymore. When they are both at home at the same time, Alex is usually asleep, trying to get some rest from all those twelve- hour shifts that he has been working. He and Donna seem to be more like two ships passing in the night. Lately, on Alex's off days, he's been trying to plan romantic dinner dates or an outing for the two of them. Donna says this isn't working for her; she's saying things like, "I need my own personal down time, some me time, so can you please quit smothering me. Why don't you go hang out with your boys, and leave me alone?"

The time has been passing pretty darn fast. It is almost graduation time for Donna once again; she tells Alex that the graduation is no big deal and asks him not to attend. Alex thinks that is somewhat strange, because when Donna received her BA, she wanted everyone there, and she could not even get enough tickets for everyone she had invited. However, Alex, being excited as well as proud of Donna, decides to give her a big surprise party anyway. Then this way, Alex thinks, he can celebrate with Donna on her biggest accomplishment to date. Alex has not checked with Donna about having the party; well, after all, it *is* a surprise for her. Somehow, it turns out to be a surprise on Alex.

First of all, Donna doesn't even show up for the party, even though Alex has been giving her lots of hints about it. Alex has been asking her all along about what time would the graduation be over, and how long after it was over would she be arriving back home. Every time Alex asks Donna any of those questions, he always has a big smile or grin on his face. But Donna, being who she is, never even takes notice of any of the hints, smiles or the big grins he had on his face, or how brightly his eyes light up when he talks about her graduation. So instead, Alex just sits there with their family and friends all evening, trying to have fun, all the while wondering where Donna could be. It just seems so strange to Alex that there is no Donna to speak of, not even a word, and she hasn't even returned any of his calls. Where is she? And what is she doing that could be so important that she hasn't gotten home, and the hour is getting later and later. He thinks maybe something had happened to her, but he is quite sure that someone would have called him, if that were the case.

Donna comes home very late that evening, after everyone has already left the party. Alex is almost finished cleaning and putting everything away from the party when she arrives home. She doesn't even notice and or care that Alex has gone through so much trouble, to make sure she would have lots of good food and fun with everyone who came. She just comes in and heads straight for the shower; once out of it, she asks Alex why he is at home, and better yet, why isn't he asleep? Alex usually goes to bed between nine and nine-thirty on his nights off, except for when he and his friends play cards. Alex can't answer her right away. He is still very angry and upset with her for being a 'no show' to her own surprise party, yet he is very relieved that she is all right. Donna goes straight to bed, with not a word as to where she has been, and or what she has been doing all evening, or why she is so late.

After a few days, when Alex can't take it any more, not knowing what had happened after her graduation, he sits Donna down at the kitchen table for a talk. Alex begins to explain to Donna about how embarrassed he was that she was a 'no-show' to her party. Then, right out of the blue, from nowhere Donna just starts screaming uncontrollably at him, "Did I ask you to give me a party? And furthermore, how much did you spend on it? Is it my fault that you misunderstand everything? No, it isn't, it is your fault that you are so dumb." Donna is still talking and yelling even louder, "Furthermore, you aren't good enough for me," and "You haven't been for a very long time. You and I travel in two different circles, and all your friends are beneath me, anyway." Then Donna says, "So why for heaven's sake would I want to spend any of my precious time with them, and definitely not on the day of my graduation? You all are losers and I don't hang out with losers. So why, Alex, would you think that I would show up at a party with you and them, when I had a chance to go to the Royal Plaza to celebrate and party for my graduation? You know, that was not even a brainteaser, it was not even something I would have ever considered. You would think that you would have given me a choice that matched up to or would top my party at the Royal Plaza. But I am noticing by the look on your face, that you were and are still too dumb to realize I will never ever take crumbs, when I can have and am due the whole cake!"

All of this is very startling and surprising news to Alex; he thought that they were all right. Donna is still shouting at him, but he is trying to think of how to make heads or tails of all that is being said. Alex can't believe that she has called him dumb, not once, but twice, without any hesitation on her part. Then it hits him like a ton of bricks and finally, Alex spoke up. "What do you mean, that I'm not good enough for you? I was good enough to marry you just out of high school, good enough to have twins by, and good enough to support us all these years. Most of all, I was good enough to work all those long hours and all the overtime I could find to pay for your BA and some of your precious Master's. Now that you have finished all your schooling, thus far, now this hardworking man is no longer good enough for you? I thought that once you graduated, we would go on a few vacations and spend some time to together and make up for all the lost times."

Donna cut right in, not letting Alex finish what he is saying. She exclaims in an even louder voice, "The only thing that is lost is you, living in your little fantasy world. I wonder what else you have been dreaming up. Not that I care or want to hear about it, for fear that I may fall asleep from sheer boredom!" Then Donna says, "Yes, and I want a divorce ASAP. I've already filed for it, so that I can get on with my life. And leave your sorry behind right here, with all your sorry friends!"

So, after all, being the kind and gentle man that he is, Alex lets Donna out of their marriage of twenty-one years. Now that they are divorced and dating other people, Donna finds herself still sexually attracted to Alex. She finally gets up the nerve and asks him one day if he would consider having sex with her. Alex agrees, because one thing is for sure, that even a blind person could see that he still misses Donna and is very much in love with her. Alex is hoping in his heart that this will lead them straight back to the altar to get married once again. Besides, he knows that when he and Donna made love in the past, they were outstanding together. It was as if they were making music together in complete harmony when they made love with each other. So now, even though they are divorced and seeing other people, they have what they call 'S dates.'

Donna has never really let Alex go; that's because she likes to toy with him. She knows that Alex is a man who loves hard and long. Never wanting to give up in his heart, Alex truly hopes that they can get back together again. Why not? His own parents have been married over forty-eight years. Why can't he and Donna get remarried and stay together forever? That is the question that haunts Alex at the very core of his soul. This is not the case for Donna; she only enjoys their encounters, but she doesn't want Alex as a husband *never ever again*. She just doesn't want to see him happy with anyone else, either, and definitely not marry another woman. It would be a disaster for her; then she may lose the grip that she has had on him for all these years.

As time goes on and a couple of years pass, Alex meets a younger woman named April, and they hit it off really well. After dating April for just a little under four months, Alex asks her to become his wife. April says yes to Alex's proposal of marriage, and the two of them get married a month later. Now Donna has gotten wind of Alex's marriage to April, and she has decided to make problems for the newlyweds. Donna is very angry with Alex because he no longer makes it for their 'S dates,' nor does he want to. So Donna begins to play her helplessness games: she knows that Alex has always been very handy, and she really doesn't know who else to call. Alex, always being the nice guy that he is, helps Donna out and fixes whatever he can, but what Donna really wants is for Alex to unstop *her* plumbing. Moreover, that's all that she really wants and it's the only thing on her mind these days.

Now Donna has started calling Alex all times of day and night, trying to put a wedge in his marriage. *Why now?* Alex begins thinking. *Thought I wasn't good enough for her.* And besides, Donna had told him they would never get married again. Somehow, Alex was always just like a puppy on a leash going to find out what is wrong and to see if he can be of any assistance. April has started getting very tired of Donna's calls, so she asks Alex not to answer Donna's calls or to help her anymore. Alex listens to April and stops. Donna is always scheming, and now she is using their sons to get hold of Alex for her. She's always asking them to find out if their dad is as happy as he says he is with April, or is he just faking and still lonely for her? She needs this information to try and break up their marriage once and for all, so that she can get what she needs and wants from Alex before April began messing with her program.

April has just found out that she's pregnant, and she can hardly wait to tell Alex the good news. April cooks a nice dinner with all of Alex's favorite foods. She calls him to find out what time he would be getting home. Alex responds by saying that the boys are in town, and they want to take their old dad out for dinner. April is sad when she hears it, knowing that she won't be able to tell Alex their big news. Besides, April knows that Alex's sons live in another state and that Alex misses them a lot, and also knows that he doesn't get a chance to see them that often. April knows that Alex is very excited because she can hear it in his voice over the phone. And that Alex would jump at any chance of getting together with them. Now she has to eat all by herself; then, after eating, she puts everything away and cleans up the kitchen before Alex comes home. Alex doesn't get in that evening until almost midnight, and he is drunk. April doesn't like when he drinks, because it makes Alex very horny. Besides, April hates when Alex's breath smells of alcohol because she knows that next, he will be breathing it all over her. She tries to act as if she was already fast asleep. But Alex still keeps bothering her until he gets what he wants, then he turns over and is fast asleep.

The next day is Saturday, and April gets up very early, as she usually does, and makes Alex his breakfast in bed. She is surprised when she goes upstairs to serve him his breakfast in bed, because Alex is up and fully dressed, all ready to go, without one word to her. April doesn't want to make a fuss about it, so she asks him, does he have time to eat? Alex says that he is sorry, and that he has promised to have breakfast with the twins this morning. Then Alex kisses her on the cheek, promising April that he will eat the breakfast that she made for him for dinner. So far, April hasn't told Alex about the pregnancy. Just as she is about to tell him, Alex is mumbling something about being late as he gives April yet another quick kiss, but this is him saying good-bye as he rushes past her. *Well, I guess I will just have to tell him later*, she thinks, while she starts to wash the dishes. Once April finishes the dishes, she goes upstairs to straighten up their bedroom, but as she begins changing the linens, she thinks she hears a strange noise and it sounds as if it is inside the house, so she goes to go see what it is.

Meanwhile, Alex has breakfast with King and Kent, and lo and behold, who but Donna walks in, acting as if it is just a coincidence that they are all there at the same time. Kent tells his dad, as Donna approaches their table, that she made them promise not to tell him that she was going to show up for breakfast. Alex says, "It's okay. I have to be getting home to do some things with April anyway." No sooner does Donna sit down then Alex stands up to go. Right away Donna asks Alex what's the rush, where is the fire? Or is it that he is so henpecked that he can't stay a few minutes longer? Well, Alex, not wanting his sons to think that way about him, sits back down. Donna knew that he would, and that's precisely why she says that to Alex. Remember, she knows him well, and she knows how to get his goat. Then Donna orders herself something to eat, while they all sit there talking.

Now it is almost one o'clock, so Alex nervously picks up his phone to call April, but before he can, Donna starts in on him again. "Have to check in every few hours, huh, Alex dear?" So Alex puts away his phone, as they're all leaving the restaurant. Donna then suggests that they go to the movies, only if Alex can stay out and play for a few more hours. "Of course I can, I can do anything that I want to do; I wear the pants in my house." Alex says this so that he can look strong in the eyes of his sons. But Donna, on the other hand, is up to no good; she is working a plan that she had put into play a couple weeks ago. She has it all together: every time Alex tries to leave, she tests and tries his manhood. She knows that he always wants to look good in their sons' eyes, no matter what it costs him in the long run. So they all go to the movies after walking around the mall with Donna, while she picks up a few things for herself, making comments like, "This is just like old times." Donna has made sure that she picked a movie that already started, so that they would all have time to play with; at least she can go shopping, which is one of her favorite pastimes.

After the movie is over, Donna tries to speak, but Alex interrupts her, telling his sons that it is time that he be heading back home and spending some time with April. After that, Alex says he had a lot of fun and that it was a very nice day, then he hugs his sons, and he leaves without another word.

When Alex arrives home, he notices that the garage door is partly opened, and he can see that April's car is still in there. Alex parks his car, goes in the house, and finds it in a big mess. Their things have been thrown around everywhere and drawers pulled out, cabinets opened. Then panic set in and he begins calling out for April. He runs upstairs to see where April is because she hasn't answered him. Alex finds April in a pool of blood, and she is barely breathing. Alex calls 911. He tells the dispatcher about April, and that he doesn't know what had happened or how long she has been lying there. The paramedics arrive in only a few minutes; the dispatcher asks Alex not to touch April because they don't want Alex to make a mistake and cause her any further harm. As soon as they arrive, they take April right to the hospital in the ambulance. Once they arrive at the hospital, April is taken straight to the operating room. She had been stabbed in the chest. Alex has been blaming himself for staying away so long, thinking that maybe it wouldn't have happened if he had been there. And furthermore, he shouldn't have let Donna rope him into an all-day and evening outing. He should have just come home right after breakfast, like he told April that he would do.

Alex is sitting down in the waiting room. He has been waiting for a few hours now; they already told him that the surgery would take a while, but now Alex is getting nervous, wanting to know how April is doing. After yet another couple of hours go by, Alex gets up because he can't take the silence and not knowing any longer. So he heads to the nurses' station to inquire as to how April is doing and how her surgery was going and how much longer it will be. The nurse tells Alex that she was just about to call for him; she then said that the surgery was kind of touch and go, and that April is now in the ICU. Then Alex asks when he will be able to see April, and the nurse asks him to wait, that they will be calling for him in a few minutes. So Alex goes to go sit back down; on his way he whispers a thank- you prayer to GOD for not letting April die. When Alex gets back to his seat, he begins thinking about how he could've prevented all of what had happened today. While he is deep in thought, Alex hears the nurse calling his name to go see his wife. Before Alex sees April, he sees all the tubes going in and out of her everywhere, all the medicines, and all the machines that are also connected to her. Alex almost faints; he has never visited anyone so sick. The doctor begins to explain to Alex about the surgery and everything that they had done to keep April alive, but they weren't able to save the baby. Alex asks the doctor, "What baby?" Then Dr. Winton tells Alex that April was four and a half months along in her pregnancy. Alex begins to cry, saying that he didn't know about the baby and that he should've been there to protect the both of them.

April is now leaving the ICU after three weeks and moving to rehab. The doctors have been telling Alex all along that April will need a lot of therapy, some of it while she's still in the hospital, then a lot more when she finally leaves and goes home.

Finally, that long awaited day has arrived for Alex, the day when he can take April home. She hasn't said much to Alex during her seven and a half weeks' stay in the regular hospital and in the rehab section. April now has to have a lot of outpatient therapy, and a nurse will visit her two to three times a week at home. Alex has been getting ready for the day when they can get back to normal, but that is still a long way away. Alex is trying to do everything that he knows to help April, but she is no longer the same woman that he married. She is very withdrawn; she doesn't talk much and never smiles or laughs with him, anymore. The doctors explain to Alex that this is to be expected and that he has to be very patient with April. They said that in most cases this is what is expected from the victim of a rape and assault. Alex is always blaming himself; he has apologized to April repeatedly for not being there. April has been home for about two months now, and her sister Ginger has come down to visit with her for a little while. Ginger told Alex that he needs to get out for a while, but he says he's not going to leave April again unless he is at work. Each day, for the few weeks since Ginger has been there, she has been trying to encourage Alex to relax and go outside and get some fresh air. "Maybe you should to go and hang out with the guys, just do something that will relax yourself." And every day, he says no to her. Until one day, April tells him to just go and get out of her sight, she is very upset and says that he should have been there when he was supposed to be. Alex is very hurt by this, so he leaves; besides, he doesn't want to upset April anymore. So he decides to go out for a bit, but not before telling her and Ginger that he will only be gone for an hour or two.

So Alex leaves the house and goes for a drive down to the gym to do a short workout, and guess who is there, too, but Donna. *Has she been following me?* he wonders. As soon as Donna spots him, she decides to go over to talk to Alex while he is lifting some weights. She starts off by saying "Hi," but Alex doesn't feel like being bothered with her and her games. So he responds with a very dry "Hi" to her and tells her to move on. She begins to tell Alex how sorry she was when she heard what had happened to April. He is screaming at her, "Who told you?" She says one of their sons did, but she can't remember which one had told her. She also says that she had said a prayer for April when she found out. Alex says, "Thanks, now that you have said what you had to say, stay away from me, and now can you please leave me and my wife alone?" Donna apologizes to Alex, then goes away with her head kind of down, making sure that he can see her.

Once Alex finishes his lifting session, he takes a shower and gets dressed, and is ready to leave the gym. On his way out. he spots Donna; she is still hanging around the gym. She asks him if he has time for a soda and some small talk. Alex tells her he doesn't have the time to spare, then she says,

"How long is the chain on your leash these days?" Alex knows that Donna is up to her old tricks, and he doesn't plan to fall for any more of them. He mans up and tells Donna that there is no leash or anything else other than he loves his wife and that he will be there for April no matter what. And to get out of his way now, because he plans to go and prepare a good home-cooked dinner for April and himself. Alex gets back home to find that while he was out, Ginger has been packing some of April's things so that April can go stay in Boston with her for a little while. April assures Alex that it will only be a short move, for a short period. Alex began to question the two of them and better yet, he wants to know from April was this always the plan, for her to leave him when Ginger came here to visit? "Haven't I told you enough times how sorry I am for not being here for you? Now you are all ready to leave me. Just when were you going to say something to me, about it? Or, did you ever plan to tell me? April, I am still your husband, right? How long have you known about leaving, or been contemplating this short move, as you have so elegantly put it?" Ginger asks Alex to please calm down and try to understand what it is like for April, being back in the same place where she had been assaulted. Ginger further explains to him that it would do April a world of good to get away for a little while. Then Alex asks April why she hadn't said something to him so that he could've taken off some time from his job to go and be with her. She tells Alex that she needs some time alone, away from their life, so she can sort everything out that has happened in the last months. Alex asks April what day are they leaving and when, how long is she planning to stay away? April tells him that the plane leaves in the morning at 7:00 a.m., and she doesn't know when she will be coming back. She then asks Alex to please trust her and to wait until she is able to return to him.

The next morning, Alex packs their suitcase in the trunk of the car and then he drives April and Ginger to the airport. Alex feels in his gut that this is a bad move, but he is willing to try and ride out this wave that had hit their lives.

April calls to say that they landed in Boston safe and sound, and that she needs to get some rest after the flight. Alex calls April back later that evening, but there is no answer, so he feels maybe they are sleep. Then he calls her back the next morning, only to hear April say that they are just leaving to go to church, and she doesn't want to be late. Alex thinks that this is kind of strange; besides, she was never in a hurry to go to church here at home. Alex tries to call April during his lunchtime that night to see how her day was, but she never answers the phone; it goes straight to Ginger's voice mail. When he gets off work, it is too early to call, so he goes home, takes a shower, and goes to bed. Alex is restless, so he gets up earlier than usual and tries to call April again; still there was no answer. Now Alex is kind of worried, but then he thinks about her therapy; maybe that's where they are. Then Alex tries to call again the next day, and the next day, and no one is returning his calls. After about two and half weeks of that, Alex is beginning to think that April has left him for good.

Then one morning, the doorbell rings, and he answers it. Once Alex opens the door, he is not too surprised to see that it is the sheriff standing there, serving him with divorce papers.

And on top of that, she wants all her things shipped to her and alimony payments on the grounds of abandonment. Alex can't believe it; he just sits down in the middle of the floor. At first, he starts feeling sorry for himself; then after a few hours, he gets kind of mad, so he calls April. This time she answers him; she tells him that she was tired of being the third wheel in their marriage. She said that if he had thought more of her and been there at home, maybe none of this would have happened to her. Then she tells him that from the start, Donna has always been in their business. Alex tries to apologize again and to explain to her about his relationship with Donna, but April says she doesn't care to hear any more excuses.

Divorced again, Alex just tries to stay close to home these days. He attends his family's church and reads his Bible a lot more since everything that happened. His friends have been trying to get him to go out and begin to date again. Then, one day, he finally gives in to the voice of his friends. Now Alex is out for the evening with his friends, and he happens to see this lady he thinks he has met before but hasn't seen for years. He tells his friends that he's sure he knows her but can't remember her name. She is very attractive and is a sharp dresser, and he just can't take his eyes off her. After his friends tease him long enough about her, Alex decides to go across the restaurant to introduce himself to her and her friends. She remembers him; she is a friend of his family, but she hasn't seen any of them for a while. Her name is Heather, and she owns her own business. Alex asks Heather how her family was doing. She tells him that her children are all grown up now, and that Mitch died five years earlier. He says he's sorry to hear that Mitch is gone. Alex tells her that she still looks the same and with those same big, beautiful, brown eyes. Heather blushes a little and says thanks and tells him that it really helps having JESUS in her life. Heather says that she attends church regularly and volunteers to help others less fortunate than herself. Alex gets so excited that he asks where her church is, right on the spot. Then he asks if it would it be okay if he visits with her sometime? She tells him the location of her church and says he is welcome to attend the different services any time that he wants to. Then Alex asks if she would consider going out on a date with him at some point in the near future. Heather says yes, then adds that she isn't sure why she said it. That makes Alex feel good; he had always thought about asking her out, but the timing was never right. He gives her his phone number and says to make sure she uses it, then returns to the table with his friends. Alex is so happy that he saw Heather again and they are both single, he smiles all the way back to his table.

Meanwhile, Donna is trying once again to get her hooks into Alex. She's been trying to get him to her house under even more false pretenses. She has been calling him at the store and going by there, trying to catch up with him. She recently broke off her engagement for the second time with her rich friend; mostly it was his choice to end it. Her friend had told her time after time not to ever make mention of, nor did he want to hear, Alex's name in his bedroom again. Donna just can't help herself; she wishes that Alex had the money and was as smart, because he is so great in the sack. When Alex shows up to help his parents at their store, lo and behold, Donna is there; she had brought his mom some perfume back from her visit to Paris. She knows how to get to him; all she has to do is just be real nice to his mother. Donna knows that Alex loves his parents, but his mother is his heart. Once Alex shows up, Donna excuses herself and leaves, assured that her plan will work. She really knows how to yank his chain, especially to get him to pay attention to her. That next week she is there at the store again, bearing gifts again for his mom. Now today, all his mom can talk about is "Donna gave me this or that, and she's always talking about how she misses you. Alex, you should give her a call. You know that you are still in love with her." Donna has worked her magic on his mom. Now his mom won't stop talking about Donna until Alex agrees to take Donna out to dinner. Feeling that there is no way out and knowing he can't ever disappoint his mom, Alex gives in, or rather, caves in to her request. So Alex calls Donna and makes a date with her for the upcoming Saturday.

It is Tuesday, and Heather calls to see if he is free on Saturday; while telling him that they are having a concert at her church, and someone just gave her a couple of free tickets. He reluctantly tells her that he already has other plans and says maybe next time. Alex feels bad, but he knows that he can't break the date, not when he has given his mom his word.

So Alex picks up Donna on Saturday for their date. They are going to see the O'Jays and the Temptations and some other groups at the Star Plaza. Dinner starts at six and the show is at seven. He has to pick Donna up at three-thirty so that he can try to beat some of the traffic headed for the concert. On the way there, Donna is testing Alex, trying to find out if she can get what she really came for tonight. Alex is her prize for the night; well, that is what she is expecting. She tells him that if he doesn't show her a good time tonight, then she will make sure his mother finds out. Now she is hugging on him and acting all sexy and romantic. She knows what he likes, and that is why she is wearing this dress. It is not missing one of her curves; she is pulling out all the stops with this outfit. Alex is trying to stay in control, but he still loves her after all these years. He just doesn't want to be hurt by her again, so he changes the topic of their conversation and pulls away. Donna, on the other hand, is not surprised by this; she has a countermove for every one of his moves. And she does plan on getting a return on her investment, whether Alex knows it or not.

Now that they have arrived, it is time to go into her little (very well planned) act; eat a tiny amount of food from the buffet and begin to feel bad. As they sit down to eat, she plays cool until it is almost time for the concert to start, then she begins to moan a little, but enough for him to hear her. "Are you all right, Donna?" he asks. She tells him that she needs to go to the ladies' room to lie down for a few minutes. Then she says for him to go on to the concert, just leave her the ticket, and she will find him when she feels better. Alex stands up to help Donna because she looks like she might fall down. Only, this is truly part of her plan; then he suggests that maybe he should take her back home, but she says no, almost immediately. What, go home and forget her well laid plan? So, Donna convinces him that she just needs to sleep it off, and all she has to do is get a room while he is at the concert, then they will leave and go straight home. Alex agrees, and so Donna goes to her room and waits for Alex to begin to worry about how she is doing.

Around an hour or so later, she hears a knock at her door to the hotel penthouse. She doesn't answer right away, so he would think that she was sleeping. After Alex has knocked a few more times, Donna opens the door for him. He apologizes for waking her up; he just wants to make sure she is okay and to see if she needs anything. She says she felt better after lying down about thirty minutes, but since she has to pay for the room, she thinks they could just stay the night. "Look, it does have two beds," she says, as she points to the bed that she was lying next to, the one he is standing right next to. Then he says, "We don't have a change of clothes." She tells him to take a look in the closet; she purchased them a set of jogging outfits and gym shoes. So he agrees to stay overnight, and then he asks her if she feels like going back to the concert with him. She says since they had already missed most of it, "Why don't you just stay here with me and we can make our own music?"

Right then, Alex knows he has been set up, but as she said, they really do make their own music whenever they are together.

It's Sunday morning about eight, and Donna is ready to have another go at it. Alex says he is hungry, and Donna says she is too, but the kitchen doesn't serve what she has a taste for on their menu. So of course, Donna gets what she wants, and now that she has gotten what she came for in the first place, she is through with him. Alex knows this because she is back to talking to him all crazy. Donna is saying things like, "Hurry up, I have a meeting to get to at three o'clock, can't you move any faster? I have to check out, you know you can't afford this room. So please go punch the button for the elevator so we can get out of this place; I have things to do, places to go, and people to meet with. And when we get to the lobby, please go and get the car so that I am not late. You know I can't go to the meeting dressed like this, don't you?" Alex is so mad, but he is not going to get into her catfight, so he just drives her home in silence. Donna, on the other hand, is making calls left and right, wheeling and dealing like there wasn't going to be a tomorrow. After he drops her off and takes her few things in for her, she tells Alex to see himself out and to lock the door because she is going upstairs to relax. Alex drives straight home, and after he gets there he heads for the shower, eats a bite and watches football the rest of the evening.

For the next week, he drags himself around the house. He has been on this self-pity trip, just staying around his house, not really going out too much for anything. He has taken a week's vacation. Now it is time for him to go back to work this evening, and he is really ready to go back. His phone starts to ring, and who is it? It is Heather. He is excited to hear her voice, but he doesn't show it. He just says hello with his deep voice and with that sound that makes women melt on the inside, so they say. Heather says hi, and then the phone goes silent, so he jokes with her. "Did you call to talk or to hold the phone?" She apologizes and asks how his day was. Then they talk for a little while, and Alex tells her that he has to get some sleep before he goes to work in a couple of hours. Then after a little while, they say their good-byes and hang up.

The next morning, he goes to see her at the place where she works after his shift ends. Alex gives her flowers, then she asks if he would like to sit down for a few minutes. So he sits down close by her, and before she knows what is happening, he pulls her close to him and gives her a quick but nice kiss. Then he says, "Call me. I will look forward to hearing from you again." Then he leaves as quickly as he showed up. As he drives away, he thinks, *I nailed that kiss; she will be mine.* Then Alex drives to his parents' store; he tries to go there at least twice a week to spend time with his parents. He has other siblings, but Alex is his mother's favorite. His mom leans on him a lot since his dad has been ill.

One month later, Heather calls him, and the first thing she asks him is, does he have time to talk to her? Alex tells her it is okay, besides, he is taking another one of his vacation weeks. Then he asks her if she is ready to go out on a date with him. Heather tells him only if it is okay with his mother. Alex laughs and says, "How do I get to know you better?" She tells him, "Come to my church, and you can see me there. "Alex says that he'd see her soon.

Alex shows up at The Clearly Saved Church, and the service has already started. Once he enters the main sanctuary, he starts looking around to see if he can spot Heather in the audience. It is a very beautiful church, with carvings of JESUS' journey walking up to Calvary on the two sidewalls. In the very front, on the whole wall, there is a very beautiful painting of CHRIST as the risen SAVIOR. Alex doesn't see Heather, so he takes a seat close to the back of the church. Not that there are any seats up much closer; he can tell that this large church is pretty packed. After the service is over, Alex asks an usher if he knows Heather Goodmore. The usher says yes, and if Alex would like, he will go get Heather for him. Alex answers yes, and the usher goes away for about three minutes, and the next time Alex looks up, he is staring into the eyes of beauty. After they greet one another, Alex asks Heather if she would like to go out to dinner. She says yes, but she has to be back for the evening service. Alex replies, "Is that all? I think that can be arranged," all the while smiling at her.

They arrive at the Uptown Diner and Café; Alex had called ahead to make their reservations while they were en route. The Uptown Diner and Café is a very fancy and upscale restaurant. Alex wants to make a great impression on Heather; that's why he brought her there in the first place. He wants to wine and dine her and show her a good time, then just maybe she will forget about going back to that church service tonight. As soon as Alex gives the waiter his name, they were seated at a nice cozy table somewhat off to the side. After they place their orders, they begin to talk, trying to get to know more about each other. They finish dinner, and their dessert has just arrived, and so has Donna. She comes by their table to say, "Hi" in a very catty territorial sort of way; Alex can see that Donna is kind of jealous, so he makes the introduction between the two of them. He introduces Donna as his ex-wife to Heather and tells Donna that Heather is a longtime friend of his family. Donna comments in a jealous tone that she knows all the old family friends, so where has Heather been hiding? Alex speaks up before

Heather can, and tells Donna to back off and allow them to finish their evening in peace. After dessert, Alex asks Heather if she would like to go to a little jazz spot since he knows that she likes it a lot. Heather declines; she explains she is already late for service, and she should be headed back there. She then thanks Alex and gives him a kiss on the cheek as she leaves the restaurant. Alex is very upset with Donna; he blames her for Heather leaving. He sees that Donna had made her very uncomfortable.

Alex calls Heather that following Tuesday to see if she is all right. She tells him that she had a nice time, but she doesn't like the threesome. Alex explains that Donna is always trying to ruin his relationships, but Heather says she rather they remain just friends and nothing else. Alex tries to persuade her to go out just once more, and if she still feels the same way, then he would do as she has said, they will just remain friends. Heather says, "All right, I will give you a chance, only this once," then she says good-bye and hangs up. He calls her right back to see if this Friday or Saturday will be okay; she says Friday. Then Alex asks would she like an intimate home-cooked meal? She says that would be just fine with her.

Now, Alex has to decide what he is going to cook Heather for their home-cooked meal, and he is very excited with all the planning.

It is Friday, and Heather is coming for dinner tonight. Alex is very nervous; he wants all to go well for him and Heather. He has been cooking all afternoon. The time has arrived, but no Heather. Alex begins to pace back and forth, wondering what has happened to her. He has tried calling, but there was no answer; now his mind is playing tricks on him. He is thinking all kind of crazy stuff, since Heather is now two hours late and hasn't returned any of his calls. Alex goes to the window to see if she might be driving up his street now, but she never shows up or calls. About ten thirty, Alex starts to put all the food away, as well as cleaning up the kitchen. Alex is very disappointed; after he finishes tidying up everything, he goes right to bed.

Alex calls Heather at seven in the morning that Saturday. He is worried about her, because she hadn't shown up for dinner. Her phone rings, then Alex hears that the voice on the other end is the voice of a male, and not Heather. He becomes upset and just hangs up. *That's why she didn't come to dinner, she was with him?* Alex is thinking all kinds of things and getting upset when his phone rings right back. He answers, and it is Heather. She asks him in a very tired voice why did he call and just hang up? Instead of answering Heather's question, he asks her why didn't she come for dinner last night or did she forget? She blurts out in tears that her mother died last evening; that is why she didn't show up for dinner. Alex begins to apologize, but Heather is crying so hard; next he hears that same male's voice as before, telling him that he might want to try back later to talk to Heather. Alex calls his mother to tell them that Heather's mom died. His mother already knows; now she asks him how he knew about it. He begins at the beginning, when he saw her at the restaurant when he was out with his friends. Then he brings her up to date with last evening's dinner and his call this morning. His mother tells him that Heather's mom has been sick for a while, and Heather was always there caring for her. His mother tells him to give Heather some time and check in on her in a couple of days. Alex is sad for Heather, but he is at a loss and he doesn't have the slightest idea of what to do, or how he can help Heather in this time in her life. Alex wants so much to be there for her.

Alex hasn't had a chance to talk to Heather, but today is her mom's funeral service, so he decides to go and see if he can be some help or some kind of support. Once there, he spots his mother, and guess who is with her, but Donna. He walks over to his mother; she is in line for the viewing. Alex wants to ask her why she brought Donna with her; she says she needed a ride, and Donna just volunteered. Donna tries to hug him, but he backs away from her; he doesn't want Heather to think he brought Donna to her mom's funeral services. After the burial, Alex stays for the repast; he finally has to get close to Heather and to extend his condolences to her. She says thanks and that she was glad he came and that it has been very hard on her, losing her mom and all. Alex asks her to call him if she needs to talk or anything, then he moves out of the way so others can talk to her.

It is three weeks since Heather's mom's funeral, and Alex still hasn't heard one word from Heather. He doesn't want to intrude, so he sends her a bouquet of flowers and the card inside that reads, *I miss you and I hope that all is well with you and I'm still here to love and support you.* Heather calls the very next day; she says, "Hi and thanks for the lovely flowers." Alex asks her if she needs anything, and she tells him that she doesn't want to come between him and Donna getting back together. Alex is shocked; he doesn't know what she is talking about. So he asks her, and she tells him that she saw them at the service together, and later she ran into Donna at the grocery store, "And Donna told me that you and she were back together." Alex tries to tell Heather that Donna is lying, but she tells him that she doesn't have time for games and says her good-bye as she is hanging up. All Alex can do is scream; he wants to strangle Donna's lying little neck.

The holidays are almost here, and Alex is feeling kind of lonely but still kind of mad at Donna for all her lies. He hasn't seen or heard from her since that funeral. Donna is probably very happy and satisfied with her lying self, hoping that she has destroyed his and Heather's chances of some kind of relationship with all her lies. She hates to see Alex with anyone, even if the person needs a paper bag over their head, so long as they are not together with Alex. Donna is willing to do anything and say anything to stop Alex's happiness; other than that, she would have to admit and agree that she was the problem in their former marriage. Now Alex has devised a plan to get Donna once and for all, to make her put up or shut up. He invites everyone over for Christmas dinner and fun, but Alex doesn't invite Donna on purpose.

Today is Christmas Day, and everything is going as planned. He has warned his sons not to tell their mom about the dinner and to make sure that it remains a secret, especially about him getting married on Christmas Day. Now the many guests are arriving at Alex's house for all the Christmas festivities and the big surprise that Alex claims will go down in his and their life history.

As the evening goes on, everyone is having fun talking and eating and enjoying themselves. Then in comes Donna; no one is surprised to see her. Donna starts looking all around to see whom she can ask questions without being obvious. Now, as soon as Alex sees Donna, he flips the script on her. He tells Donna that he is so happy to see her, and that he's been anticipating her arrival. Donna does not know how to respond to that statement. She has no idea that everybody has been waiting for her arrival. Alex asks her what has taken her so long to get there. Now, Alex is assuring Donna that everything is all right and it's time to proceed with the wedding as planned. Donna hasn't a clue as to what is going on. She trying to understand and to keep focus, yet she is still looking around for Heather. She still thinks that Heather is the one Alex is marrying. Donna has no clue that *she* is the bride-to-be; she has been trying to ask, but everyone thinks that she is joking. The joke is truly on her this time, because she has crashed one party too many, and now she has crashed her own renewal.

Alex stands up in a chair to get all their guests' attention, then he says, "Sorry for the long wait, but the bride has finally arrived and now we can get on with the saying our vows. You know, they say that the second time around is a great thing." Now Donna is getting kind of nervous, and what and who is Alex talking about? Alex's mother tells Donna to go on up to the front and get her man, and that they are so glad that they both have come to their senses. Donna is speechless; the many excited guests are pushing her lightly to the front. When she gets up to the front, she asks Alex what is going on. He whispers in her ear that he realizes that she wants to be with him and that is why she has been sabotaging his relationships, so he has decided that they should renew their vows. At this point, Donna is furious with Alex; then she looks up, and their sons come out to give her away to their dad, and they are as happy as they can be. Then the minister steps out in front of them and begins his speech, you know, the one they always do, and before anyone can think, Donna runs out the door lightning fast, and Alex begins laughing. When he stops laughing, he explains to his many guests what had just happened and that he could now go on and have a real life without any more of Donna's involvement anywhere. After the initial shock, everyone has a good laugh and continues with the rest of the Christmas festivities.

Chapter Five

Valencia

Valencia is a fictionalized character who was taught by her parent that it is all right to accept rejection and abuse with open arms and not to fight against it.

As if growing up in the back woods of Mississippi wasn't hard enough, I had very little contact with people other than school and church. My mother always told me to hurry home from school so that I could help with chores and everything else she had for me to do. This caused me to be a loner. At school, I didn't have much to say. When anyone tried to invite me to their parties, my mother would say okay, but then she would always make sure that I never made it to them. After a while, the other children just stopped inviting me altogether.

I was always told, and reminded relentlessly, that I would never amount to anything. My mother reminded me constantly that even with my beauty and nice shape I could get a man, but that he would never be faithful to me. I often wondered why and how my mother could make such negative statements about me, especially being her own flesh and blood. One day, I decided to ask her, why? Why did she say those things about me? Didn't she want me to succeed and live a happy life? The next thing happened within an instant. I felt her hand; it had swung back so fast and with such fury. It hit me in the mouth, busting my lip and knocking me to the floor instantly before I knew that I was hit or what had happened to me. Then my next memory after that was all the pain that I felt throbbing from my face and in my mouth. Then all I heard her saying was, "Don't you never ever try and sass your momma; I'll take you out of here. Now, you just get up from that floor there and listen to me! And I don't want to hear one earthly thing come out of your mouth." As I pulled myself up into the chair that was closest to me, I still wondered why. Why did she hit me and why couldn't I have the man of my dreams like in the movies? My mother was still speaking as I sat up, and furthermore, she said, "And you'd better keep working hard at your job and have plenty of babies for him. That's the only way to keep a man because beauty and shapes fade away. And the most important thing to remember is when he starts having other women, you act like you don't know nothing about nothing. You keep his house clean, and make sure you cook three hot square meals a day, keep them babies clean and out of his way, and give him as much sex as he wants and as often as he wants. Now you lock that in your memory and don't you never forget it, or you will suffer and pay dearly."

After dad died, we moved up north, to Chicago, Illinois. We stayed with my aunt for a little while until we found a nice house of our own on the west side of town. We had to do all our moving on the weekend, so that I wouldn't miss going to work on Monday morning. I was always glad to go to work to get away from the house and momma for a while. She always had something or other for me to do around the house every waking moment; nothing was ever good enough and nothing was ever done. She would always find something for me to do, especially if I had plans to go somewhere or do something outside of the house. There was never enough money to really enjoy myself because my mother had already made plans for it: my raise, my check, my money. I didn't get out very often and I hadn't had many dates because Momma didn't approve of the different suitors.

When I met Steven, Mother was crazy about him. After we had dated for a brief period of time, it wasn't long before Steven asked me to marry him, and I immediately said yes. At that time, all I really knew about Steven was that he had graduated from college, and he had a good job at this medical supply company with the potential of becoming the regional manager in the next year or so. I was happy, no matter what. I was glad to be out of that house and that life for good, or was I? I thought that I had escaped from my mother, but Steven would always invite her over. He loved how she always made sure I was being a good wife and taking care of him, the King, at all cost. Every time she came over for a visit, I always dreaded them because the only thing she told me was how to treat Steven better. Never once did she ask me how Steven was treating me. She just kept telling Steven that Valencia can work harder, and Valencia knows how to keep her mouth shut and keep these babies quiet so you so can rest. Why would my mother do that to me? Then I would remember the words that she told me many years ago as if 'they' were an unspoken commandment that I had to remember to always follow and accept without one word and never say anything in my own defense. I had met a couple of people outside of church and we were becoming close. I would say that we were friends. I dared not mention them to my mother. Whenever we got together, we had lots of laughs and fun and for a while, all my troubles would be behind me. Steven never seemed to mind my friends; he acted as if he were glad that I had them.

Steven was always on the go here and there; he hardly ever stayed at home. On Monday nights, he played cards. Wednesday nights he attended midweek service at The Great Starlight MB Church, that was where we fellowshipped. Then on Fridays, Steven said he has to work late, sometimes until three and four in the morning. I used to attend church with him on Wednesday nights, but not since we had these three children. Steven said that they make too much noise, and it took too long for us to get ready, so he just went to service all by himself. One thing I didn't understand is why Steven never made it back from midweek service until ten thirty or eleven, when service was always over by eight-fifteen. When Steven and I attended services together, we arrived home by ten to nine, and that was with us socializing a little bit after service. We only lived twelve minutes from the church, and if the weather was bad, it took us about eighteen minutes to get home. If I asked Steven why he was late, he told me to shut up before he did something that I would regret.

Steven was so sweet to the people around the church, and he was always so helpful, especially taking the women home who didn't have a car or a way home. There was this one single lady, Sister Backstabber, at our church that Steven was now telling that he would drop me and the kids off first, and she was to wait for him, and he would be right back to take Sister Backstabber home. One day, I asked Steven why didn't Sister Backstabber ride in the van with the rest of us, just like the other women did? He told me that Sister Backstabber was a real 'lady,' and he didn't want her in the van with us, meaning me and our kids. Steven would rush us to get out of the van, not caring or even thinking about helping with the children, and most definitely not waiting to see if we got into the house safe. Steven would just speed off, seemingly burning rubber, as he drove away, and Steven never just came right back. He always said he had to help Sister Backstabber to do something or another. He never helped me with anything. With Steven being a deacon at the church and all, he was supposed to help all those in need, right? But, what about helping me? I was his wife, didn't charity start at home, then spread abroad?

One Thursday evening, our phone rang, and Sister Backstabber was on the other end. I asked her what she needed; then Sister Backstabber told me to shut up and just give Steven the damn phone, which I did. Steven always told me to ask what they wanted, but if they didn't want to say why they were calling, just give him the phone. When Steven hung up the phone, he started to put his shoes and jacket on, at the same time asking where the keys to the van were. I tried asking Steven what Sister Backstabber wanted with him and where was he going? Steven just told me that he forgot to do something, and with that, Steven was out the front door and driving away.

He came back about two in the morning. I was still up, thinking about Steven and Sister Backstabber and what they were doing all that time. I tried not to think about Steven having sex with her, but I knew it was a great possibility. Steven had already said he didn't want me that way anymore; he just wanted my paycheck. Besides, we hadn't been intimate regularly for a long time. I could hear my mother, may GOD rest her soul, telling me never to question Steven about where he went and what he was doing, just be glad that he came back home to me. I think my mother told me all that so that I would stay married until truly death do us part. The same way she and my father stayed together, with no questions asked. My father used to be down to Sister White's house all the time, and my mother said that it was okay. But before my dad started hanging out at Sister White's house, he hung out at Sister So-and-so's house, and others before her and then he was gone from everyone, he died.

I ran and jumped in the bed and pretended to be sleeping when I saw the lights from our van pulling into our driveway. Steven had told me never to wait up for him and that I needed my rest so that I could be fresh every day that I had to go into work. That was so considerate of Steven, even though he never helps out with anything at home. I continued to cook and clean and take care of the kids like my mother always told me to do and never ask Steven any questions.

After a few years of that, I wanted us to seek help with our marriage. I arranged for us to meet with our pastor, Pastor Goodhearted. I wanted the both of us to sit down and to talk to the pastor, hoping for some much-needed help and to get some kind of counseling. Somehow, Steven got wind of it before I could talk to him about it. He became very angry. Steven threatened me with leaving me and our children, if I said anything else or tried to press the issue. Then Steven started calling me ugly and making up fat jokes about me. I ended up crying most of the time, with him laughing very hard and telling me I was a fool. That caused me never to bring up that conversation ever again. The memory of it and Steven made me feel so discouraged and lonely. I would talk to my friends, but I never told them everything that was going on; they probably already knew what was going on. People in our church circle were always talking about this or that. I have always feared having to raise our children all by myself. I needed to always remain Mrs. Steven Givens, no matter what the cost or shame that I would have to bear. Be it in private or out in public, I was still the one who Steven had married, not them. So I withdrew, in my heart, the feelings and emotions that I had for Steven. I just began to shower even more love on our children, and I started living only to see their dreams come true. I thank GOD for my friends; they help me a lot. I continued to do my duties keeping the house clean, cooking three hot meals a day, and making sure the kids were clean and quiet, never ever disturbing Steven.

Steven and I had been married twenty-one years, and Steven was now the pastor of The Great Starlight MB Church. Our former pastor, Pastor Goodhearted, died three years ago, and the deacon board, and then the congregation, voted Steven in as the new pastor. Steven had always said that he knew that he would be a pastor one day. Since Steven had held this position of being the pastor, he was hardly ever home. I didn't know what Steven did, and most the time I didn't even care to ask, but I prayed things would get better for me, Steven, and our family.

Steven's newest interest was the head of the pastors' aid committee, Sister Stealer. I heard that Sister Stealer had other male companions besides Steven, but that Steven didn't seem to mind. Lately, our church had been having some kind of different afternoon service or other. I hardly ever attended the afternoon services. On this one particular Sunday afternoon, I was in attendance. I went to the ladies' bathroom; it was empty when I entered my stall. But no sooner that I had locked the stall door then in came two of the sisters at church. Sister Meddlesome was talking to Sister Busybody, and they always knew something about everybody else's business. And now they were discussing it in the bathroom. They really didn't have any personal business to do in the ladies' bathroom. They just had to make sure their latest stories and information were straight. I didn't think that they knew that I was in the bathroom, or maybe they didn't care, so I stayed in my stall, just listening. Trying to be very still and quiet, but to make sure I heard what they had to say about the latest gossip around the church. Sister Busybody and Sister Meddlesome both agreed and said that some of the women in the church were giving the pastor, my Steven, money in his hand instead of putting it in the offering. They also said that they heard it from a reliable source of Sister Busybody's. She said that Steven gave most of that money from the other women to Sister Stealer. They said Sister Stealer in turn gave Steven sexual favors, but only when Sister Stealer had the time away from her other male partners. Sister Meddlesome and Sister Busybody said that Sister Stealer and Steven had been seen traveling around town a lot together lately, doing only GOD knew what and that Steven and Sister Stealer were going to have to answer to GOD for 'all' of it. *They don't know that they have to answerer for all their gossip, do they?* Then Sister Busybody asked Sister Meddlesome did she know that Sister Stealer always met the pastor up at the church? Always lying about having church business to attend to. That was the way they got to do all sorts of things together without raising any suspicions among the church folks. Sister Meddlesome and Sister Busybody continued to talk, while making even more accusations, for a little while longer, then Sister Meddlesome and Sister Busybody laughed and left the bathroom. But I stayed in that stall until I knew Sister Meddlesome and Sister Busybody were gone for sure, then I came out. I just whispered a prayer, asking God to watch over Steven, and I went back into church because the service was still going on.

Once, the members had a picnic at the church, and Sister Stealer came in looking whipped. She went over to talk to Steven, and right away on the spot Steven reached in his pocket and shoved money into her hand and said, "Go fix yourself up." Steven got mad if I didn't look good, and he said that our children must always look presentable. You know it was only for appearances, since he was the big-time pastor now. Those sisters at the church were always in his office cleaning up and giving manicures and pedicures to him. He said that that was how everyone should treat their pastor. I began to question myself as to why couldn't Steve just go to a nail salon and get his manicure and pedicure? The people were supposed to take good care of him, him being their pastor and all. He also promised that he would take good care of them, the sisters of the church.

"I'm a man with a lot of jobs, and they cause me to have to perform many duties, and besides, they allow me certain perks, if you know what I mean. How else do you think I can take care of you?" Steven quit his job a year after he became the pastor; he said that the people needed him to be available anytime, day or night. Steven preached very hard on Sundays, and the people loved him to pieces, especially all those pieces that he gave to a particular woman or women of his choice, which certainly did not include me. There wasn't anything that some of them wouldn't do for him; I saw it all the time. They bought Steven all kinds of suits and everything else, even down to his underwear. He told me to keep my mouth shut about what they do, and don't ask him nothing about nothing. Steven reminded me of my mother when he said that. Then Steven told me how blessed I was that he stayed married to me all these years. Really, like Steven had done some great deed for me; must be that selective memory that he always had. He only remembered what he wanted to, even if it was made up by him telling himself a lie and then believing it as if it were GOD's honest truth in his mind by and for himself. I had truly been the one supporting Steven and our children for all these years, or did he just forget? I doubt that, but then again, Steven worked about ten different good and odd jobs during our marriage before he stopped, or got fired, or was let go for drugs or something else. That they were jealous of him. Or, just Steven talking and telling about me his big dreams or another of his 'get rich quick' schemes all the time.

Our twenty-fifth wedding anniversary is approaching, and I am not so excited about it as I would be if things were different with me and Steven.

Our three adult children have discussed it among themselves and they want us to have a big celebration. Steven has agreed to it; I don't know why he has agreed to it and I dare not ask for fear of rocking some kind of boat. There is something different about him these days, but I don't know what it is. I just continue to pray, asking the Lord daily to help direct Steven in all of his life and our lives and his decision makings, and to please take control of his heart and mind for him as always. Our children have started planning all the festivities for my and Steven's big day; they are so excited that they will be in attendance this time, since they weren't even born the first time around. I am kind of relieved my mother is not here to be part of the upcoming renewal; besides, she might think it doesn't call for all that. The date has been set for August 3, at four o'clock in the afternoon at the Fritz Chapel and Banquet facilities. I am so excited with the thought of Steven wanting us to renew our vows. I believe this time Steven really wants to do right by me. Lately, Steven has been staying closer to home, and he's even started to act as if he might love me. I've been wondering, is it all real; one day, I even pinched myself to check and see if I was awake and that all of this was really happening to me. Steven wants to take me shopping for my clothes for our renewal. Steven has asked me to help him find everything that he will need for our renewal as well. I've always picked out his clothing: that's one of the things that has been the same since we got married, other than when those women at church bought clothes for Steven. But this time is very different and very pleasant; Steven asked me would I help him. He said that he wanted and welcomed my suggestions as to what he should wear to our renewal. He made me feel that I, and my opinions, mattered to him. I haven't seen that side of him in years. I feel that maybe, and I'm really hoping, Steven is trying to make amends in our relationship. I've always felt like a third wheel and an old shoe for most of our marriage. The big day is only a week away, and Sister Stealer has continued nonstop; every day she keeps calling Steven, and he hasn't responded to her like he did in past times. She has been very angry and yet very scarce around the church for a couple of weeks. Whenever she does show up, she only comes to speak to Steven in private. Last Sunday, she said in one of her many outbursts that we were going to do this over Steven's dead body, if we were determined and insisted on going forward with this mess. I could not imagine she was calling our renewal a mess, but didn't GOD say in Matthew 19:6 what therefore HE has joined together let no man put asunder? Our children told me that they were kind of worried about what Sister Stealer might be calculating in her evil mind to do, so they asked me to talk to their father about their concerns. Steven in turn told them not to worry and that it is all under control. That was something even I needed to believe.

On the morning of August 3, Steven did something he hadn't done in years: he went out to pull the trash, without being asked, and took it to the curb. I was looking out the window, watching Steven and feeling pleased inside that our lives were turning in the same direction. Only to see that when Steven reached the curb, Sister Stealer drove up very fast and then jumped out her car and begins to open fire on Steven, hitting him in the upper parts of his body. I screamed and ran outside. As I was approaching Steven, Sister Stealer aimed her gun at Steven once more, and she fired yet another bullet into him. Steven was falling to the ground, in what seemed like slow motion, which took an eternity. Then Sister Stealer just climbed into her car after that. I heard yet another gunshot. I later found out from the police that she shot herself in the head after shooting Steven. All I could see was a lot of blood. I could also hear the different sirens in the background as I kneeled down and lifted Steven's head. He was trying to say something, so I got closer to him. Speaking a little above a whisper, Steven said he had broken it off with Sister Stealer a few months ago. Then Steven told me that he was so sorry for how he had treated me all these years. Steven said that I was a good wife and mother, but he didn't know how to treat a good woman. I told Steven to hush and that I had forgiven him a long time ago. After that, Steven's eyes closed. At that same time, I felt someone pulling at me, saying, "Miss, we need you to move back so that the paramedics can try and help him." When I looked up to see who was speaking, it was a nice police officer. His name is Officer Compassion, the one who patrols the school grounds down the street from our house. As Officer Compassion was leading me away from where Steven was lying on the ground, he asked me what happened and if I saw anything. I was crying so hard, but I told him everything that I saw, but that everything happened so fast I couldn't stop it. Officer Compassion told me that I was blessed that she didn't start shooting at me. Officer Compassion said the best thing to do when someone starts shooting is to take cover. I told Officer Compassion that Steven was my husband, and I needed to make sure he was okay. The paramedics were putting Steven in the ambulance. I asked if I could ride with them to the hospital, but Officer Compassion interrupted, he said that he would drive me to the hospital.

After I got into the squad car, we headed for the hospital, which was two miles away. I felt numb, but I was still praying on the inside, asking for GOD's mercy for Steven. Then my thoughts quickly turned to our children and how I was going to tell them what happened to my husband and their father. When we finally arrived at Safe Haven Hospital, I asked how Steven Givens was and when could I see him. The nurse told me to please have a seat and that the doctor would be out to see me in a few minutes.

Finally, when the doctor came out to see me, I jumped up from my chair and I hesitantly asked him how Steven was doing. The doctor told me that Steven was DOA. I began screaming, but nothing came out my mouth, the screaming was deep down inside of me. Then they took me in to view Steven's body. When I saw Steven lying on that table, at that moment I noticed that he looked so peaceful. The only thought that came into my mind was, *Now it really is over.* Then under my breath, with a lot of love, I whispered a final good-bye to Steven, the man whom I had loved for over twenty-five years. I will miss Steven, but I thank God for that moment we had in the end.

Chapter Six

The Broken Vessel

Here we have a very beautiful priceless glass, and we've taken all the care in the world to make sure that it stays as lovely as it was that day when we first attained it, carefully cleaning it and replacing it in its protective case. What happens when this priceless glass gets chipped, unknowingly to us, or, for goodness' sake, it gets broken? This is something that we never thought of, or even wanted to imagine: that such a thing could become the fate of our treasure. Not only that, we weren't ready, not prepared, nor are we equipped to handle it. Now we have to make a rational decision; do we keep it or do we throw it away? Perhaps the chipped piece can be fixed? But no matter how we try, we can't fix it in its broken state. At least, not back to the way it was when it was so alluring to us and it was the center of our pride. Always showing it off to this or that person, getting even more praise and compliments on how beautiful it is. So now what do we do about it? Do we ignore it, or do we just discard it? Perhaps with a glass we can do this, but this is not the solution for a person when they are chipped or broken: they can't just be thrown away.

Unfortunately, this is what happens to those whom we once loved. We soon forget that they were once the center of our joy, and that they made our hearts feel warm, and we wanted to sing their praises to the world. For some reason or another, we even pledged them our undying love and protection. Oh, but now we say that was in the past, we don't care for them now. Did we really care about them, or were they just a passing fancy for us for the time? No, we just outright rejected them, no matter what the cost, "We are done, and we are finished," even if we have to inflict more pain on them to get rid of them. Is this how GOD did us? No, HE loved us, even when we didn't love ourselves. HE gave HIS only BEGOTTEN SON for us. To die in our place, JESUS became the perfect sacrifice for us all.

We have become so familiar with the spirit of rejection, we just take off one piece of rejection's clothing and put on another one. We never stop and think to check to see if there is a loose button, a snag in the material, or a stuck or broken zipper. It's like we are dancing in the dark and changing dance partners, never familiarizing ourselves with them. Just dancing to the tune of this or that song until the music stops.

People are always rejecting something or another, and yes, we even reject and abuse each other. Yes, we intentionally throw the baby out with the bath water, with no remorse or even a thought as to how they will feel or what will become of them. Do we even care? Forget them all; we have decided to move on, now it's time to change our phone number, address, and even our church, just so we can be rid of and ignore this person whom we once loved and had to have so desperately. What happened? We act as though they weren't a real, breathing person. What if GOD had rejected us, like we did that person or those people whom we loved so much at first, or did we ever love them? No, 'forget' them. We do what we do, and we are good at it and proud of it. We tell ourselves, "Somebody hurt me, and I survived." Or did we really just psych ourselves out? Saying they, the one who we rejected, didn't matter anyway, they just seriously need to develop a thicker skin and quit wearing their feeling on their sleeves. The rejected should get over themselves and begin to live in the real world. Put away their fantasies and stop all this stupid daydreaming. They should know nothing lasts forever, and besides, we have to move on to greener pastures.

So we ignore their pain, leaving them to patch up their many wounds. If we are really good at hurting people, and without any feelings, we would just go on as if they really didn't exist at all in the first place. Thanks, but no thanks. Perhaps we went as far as to trade up for money and or fame. Well, that's all good and well for the perpetrator, but what about the one who was abused? No doubt it was crushing and very devastating to them. They are now wondering, "Why, why? What should I have done differently or better?" NOTHING! ABSOLUTELY NOTHING AT ALL! They were truly given the short end of the stick.

I'll tell you, for the abused, it is like a storm passing over, or a tornado with three or four twisters when the relationship comes to an end. You look around to find that you have been rejected once again for one of the thousand lame excuses and reasons. None of which you were led to believe at first. You ask the question, "Will my heart hold up through this, this time?" Yes, it will. Will your mind stop playing those same old words, pictures, thoughts, and places over and over again? Yes, it will. The answer to this and all the other questions that you may have can be found in the WORD of GOD. 2 Corinthians 10:4-5 tells us:

> " [4] For the weapons of our warfare are not carnal, but mighty through God to the pulling down of strongholds;
>
> [5] Casting down imaginations, and every high thing that exalteth itself against the knowledge of God, and bringing into captivity every thought to the obedience of Christ;…"

We must begin the development of our real selves, our soul. The soul is the part of you that is meant to live throughout all eternity.

First, you need to understand that you can and will make it. All you have to realize is that it has all been a setup from the enemy (satan), to destroy you and your seed(s). St. John 10:10 says:

"The thief cometh not, but for to steal, and to kill, and to destroy: I am come that they might have life, and that they might have it more abundantly."

Listen up and pay attention: you are strong, and you must continue to fight to live to stay above all that has tried to kill you. Psalm 118:17 states:

"I shall not die, but live, and declare the works of the LORD."

You can change it and stop this vicious cycle once and for all, through GOD (THE FATHER, THE SON, and THE HOLY SPIRIT). HE is the only ONE

who has and knows the plans for your life. Jeremiah 29:11-13 says:

" [11] For I know the thoughts that I think toward you, saith the LORD, thoughts of peace, and not of evil, to give you an expected end.

[12] Then shall ye call upon me, and ye shall go and pray unto me, and I will hearken unto you.

[13] And ye shall seek me, and find me, when ye shall search for me with all your heart."

The only thing you have to do is accept JESUS CHRIST as the LORD over your life. You know, what I found out one day was that if I didn't make the choice for myself, that satan is the lord over my life. He chooses you whether or not you want him (satan) to be over your life. So if you don't make the choice, the choice has been made for you. So here is a pointer to point you in the right direction: Romans 10:9 says:

"That thou shalt confess with thy mouth the LORD JESUS, and shalt believe in thine heart that GOD hath raised HIM from the dead, thou shalt be saved." Now, remember this: CHRIST only comes into your life to help you. HE helps you through HIS WORD. So you must begin to renew your mind with the WORD of GOD. By reading the WORD on a daily basis as often as you eat a natural meal to fill your stomach, please feed and fill your soul with HIS WORD. Romans 12:1-2 says:

> " [1] I beseech you therefore, brethren, by the mercies of God, that ye present your bodies a living sacrifice, holy, acceptable unto God, which is your reasonable service.
>
> [2] And be not conformed to this world: but be ye transformed by the renewing of your mind, that ye may prove what is that good, and acceptable, and perfect, will of God."

You must change how you think because, contrary to what you or others may think, this situation did not happen overnight, and it will not just disappear in one or two nights. It took time for you to get into the shape that you are in, and it will take some time to reverse the situation. But I can promise you this: if you will give yourself some time in the WORD of GOD, it will begin a change in you. And once you begin to change from the inside out, the things, person, and or people that brought you to this road will no longer have the effect or control that they once had in and over your life. Hallelujah! Psalm 103:1-5 says:

> " [1] Bless the LORD, O my soul: and all that is within me, bless His holy name.
>
> [2] Bless the LORD, Oh my soul and forget not all His benefit;
>
> [3] Who forgiveth all thine iniquities; who healeth all thy diseases;
>
> [4] Who redeemeth thy life from destruction; who crowneth thee with loving kindness and tender mercies;
>
> [5] Who satisfieth thy mouth with good things; so that thy youth is renewed like the eagle's."

See that rejection comes from the enemy, satan, and satan is not human, he is a fallen angel. We must begin to learn more of the WORD so that we can understand the real reason behind all that we have gone through and yet still may be going through. To know once and for all the source that is behind all your hurt and pain, even though you allowed it and gave power to it over yourself. I know that it's no fun to admit that we had a hand in some of what has happened to us. But now that we have some knowledge and some understanding about us and them, we can begin to protect ourselves. Ephesians 6:12-18 says:

> " 12 For we wrestle not against flesh and blood, but against principalities, against powers, against the rulers of the darkness of this world, against spiritual wickedness in high places.
>
> 13 Wherefore take unto you the whole armor of God, that ye may be able to withstand in the evil day, and having done all, to stand.
>
> 14 Stand therefore, having your loins girt about with truth, and having on the breastplate of righteousness;
>
> 15 And your feet shod with the preparation of the gospel of peace;
>
> 16 Above all, taking the shield of faith, wherewith ye shall be able to quench all the fiery darts of the wicked.
>
> 17 And take the helmet of salvation, and the sword of the Spirit, which is the word of God:
>
> 18 Praying always with all prayer and supplication in the Spirit, and watching thereunto with all perseverance and supplication for all saints;"

No matter what road or path that you have taken in life on purpose or whether it was by force, let me assure you that GOD is able to deliver you and set you free from any prison that you may be in. Whether it has thick iron bars, razor and barbed wire, with the state-of-the-art security, or you are in a prison that you have built in your mind and heart. There are no doors that are locked that cannot be opened. God has the key to unlock those doors and free you of everything that is binding you. We know that life has taken you down many roads. And you may have made a few wrong turns.

Does that mean it is over, and that you are all washed up? No, it doesn't, and no, you are not.

When we go on our many journeys of life, there are rules and regulations and signs we must follow. As a traveler on the road of life, we make right and left turns. Some of the turns that we took may have been the wrong ones, but we made them, no doubt. Now our lives are coming to an intersection and the lights are flashing. Upon our approach, we hear a small voice on the inside that cautions us, so we begin to push on our brakes and slow down. This is a must, so we don't just jump out there; if we don't stop right there, we'd get in an accident. As we proceed on this road of life, it throws us a curveball. We then end up taking a turn that we weren't aware of, nor were we prepared for it. Now we must pull over to the side of the road to what we deem a safe spot, and STOP and try to make a decision, right or wrong. The many different signs state that there is some construction going on up ahead. We must take an observation of all that is happening: one sign says ROAD ENDS UP AHEAD. Another says DEAD END. Still another says NO LEFT TURN. Then you spot a sign, and it says DETOUR. How were you able to go on so far in life if you weren't able to see these many signs? What happened? Did you see the signs and just ignore them? I'll tell you some good news: that GOD has made an escape for you in HIS WORD.

When I first started on this project, I didn't think that I could do it. And furthermore, who was I, telling people that they have been rejected and or abused? However, as these words formed on the many pages of this book, I began to see myself with this mirrored experience; I have cried and cried. But as time would have it, I can now laugh. I have found out and know for certainty that the joy of the LORD is truly my strength. Please read Neh. 8:10. Please allow the deliverance to take place in your life. You don't have to be ashamed to cry; tears shed are not because you are weak, they are to wash and cleanse your soul. They can help you begin the healing process, which will cause you to become strengthened. When you allow GOD to pour HIS love in and on you, in time you will see the things that are wrong in your life change. It will not be because the things or circumstances in your life have changed, it will because you have changed through the power of GOD's love. I pray that you will take heed and pay strict attention to what I am telling you. GOD has done wonders with and in my life, and HE is yet molding and fashioning me, yes, me, so that I will be fit for The Master's use.

Let me start by telling you that I too have been abused. This has been something that I didn't want to hear about, or for anyone to know about me. But in order to keep myself free and to help others to become free from the bonds of the spirit of rejection, I must tell my story. When I first realized that I had been abused, I had to accept that I was broken. I was saved and spirit-filled and in love with the LORD and HIM loving me.

One night, the HOLY SPIRIT took me back to when I was five years old, and I saw myself being molested by friends of the family. The lady and man got me out of my bed and took me to a back bedroom. They took turns holding me up over this very large can with the top halfway opened; it had really jagged sharp edges. All the time they were holding me, I kept squirming. I was told that if I didn't stop moving, they were just going to let me go to fall on the can, at the same time reminding me that I could get cut up really bad on the can behind the door. This went on for a long time until we moved away from that place.

One time when this abuse was still going on, my younger brother and I were playing hide and seek. It was always dark in that back area of the house in the evening. So after my brother hid, I started to look for him. I had searched everywhere else in that large apartment but that one room. I dreaded going into that room to look for him, so instead, I pushed the door open as hard as I could, not knowing that my brother was hiding directly behind the door. On that day the can was there, and I didn't know it. The next thing that I heard was him screaming. He had fallen back on the can and got cut up bad. I was blamed for putting the can there and causing him to get hurt on it. I tried telling everyone that I didn't put that can behind the door, without telling them the real truth as to why the can was there in the first place. I was told by these two friends of the family that they were going to kill all of us if I ever told anyone what they were doing to me at night when everyone else was asleep. So I got a really bad whipping for that and was even accused of putting the can there for years. Never ever able to tell my side of that horrible time in my life.

When the HOLY SPIRIT showed me this, I balled up in a fetal position and began to cry so hard. For years, I was blamed for placing that can behind the door. I always knew in my heart that it wasn't my fault that he had gotten hurt. After a long period of time had gone by, I could no longer remember how that can really got there; maybe I just blocked out the pain of it all. Because no matter as hard as I tried to remember the real details of what really happened back then, I couldn't remember any of it. I would always just say that I didn't do it, and in my heart, I knew I couldn't have done that to my brother.

Through the years of my life, I received a lot of whippings, mainly for asking why, about anything, and because I was told I was bad. I found out that that wasn't the truth either. Sometimes when you have a broken and rejected parent, they will, without realizing it, abuse you. They can cause you to become even more broken than they are. I used to cry a lot when I was younger for just about any and everything. Especially when I was told that I was adopted and or that they, my siblings just found me in the streets and brought me home. As I got older, it would still hurt me a lot, until one day, I didn't care one way or the other about how I got to be part of my family.

Unaware of the pain that I was really in, I gave the spirit of rejection a bigger hold on my life. This particular spirit helped me to hide my pain of being broken and to become an abuser in my early twenties. From that time on, if you thought about hurting me, I would hurt you first. Yes, I was a very kind person with a good heart, but very broken on the inside. I would help anyone, especially women and children. Mainly the help was for the children; I didn't want any child to suffer any abuse and to feel like I had felt for years. So if it was any way possible and within my power to help them, I would do so with no questions asked. But I couldn't and wasn't going to stand for anyone inflicting any more pain on me or in my life.

I have done some things in my life that I am not proud of and I now regret. I used to wish I could change them, but when we look at the roads that we have taken in life, we can't change them and can't, on our own, make them right. If that were the case, why would we ever want or need a SAVIOR? But the WORD of GOD has made the crooked ways in my life straight, and HE can help you get your life in order as well. (Read Isaiah 45:2.) I know that I am now forgiven of all my past sins and unrighteousness. I've learned to repent every day before I pray for all the sins that I have committed in thought, word, and deed. I have found this to be a good thing to do, as long as you mean it. You mustn't and cannot continue as the old man, the person you were before HIM, before accepting Christ in your life, and that was when you, on your own and with your free will, received and accepted CHRIST into your life. The WORD of GOD says that old things are passed away and behold all things become new (2 Cor. 5:17). They are now covered by the BLOOD of JESUS, and GOD has cast them into the sea, as far as the east is from the west, He has removed our transgressions as in Psalm 103:12, and they are remembered no more. This, to me and for me, is a wonderful thing, that 'my' JESUS has done this just for me. You see, I take it personally because GOD is into personal relationships. The LORD deals with each person one on one and HE desires to have a personal relationship with you. So, I will not allow anyone to bring up any parts of my past to me, and I am especially not going to listen to the very enemy of my soul, which is satan himself.

Now, as I began to look at my life and other lives that were broken, I know that we all have to make the right choice to accept CHRIST into our many broken lives. CHRIST has been the source of our deliverance and the glue that holds us together. This, strangely enough, puts in my mind a stained-glass window. When you first look at it, you see the different colors and you see the many pictures that are designed into this stained glass. Did you ever stop to think that something had to be broken to make it so beautiful? Did you pay attention to the black lines in between all of the broken glass pieces? I feel that it is some type of bonding glue, to somehow hold it altogether. That is what the FATHER GOD did for us by sending JESUS to hang, bleed, and die for us, then to be resurrected, and now HE lives, and we live in HIM. We have been broken on purpose to help someone else on this journey and give them the same hope we have in CHRIST JESUS. The WORD in Luke 22:32 says when you are converted, strengthen your brethren. We are always to help and not wound people, seeing that we were once wounded ourselves.

Now I have the privilege of giving you a gift that was expressed to me. I was very honored to receive it on your behalf.

It is forever, and it is for everyone who is reading this book.

My Dear Child:

Whatever that has happened to you, there is an answer, and there is a solution to the mishaps in life. And for whatever you may have felt and had to endure, LOVE says to you, I stand today with my arms stretched out wide. I have had them stretched out for over two thousand years just for you. And with all the love that I have had for you throughout all the ages of time and for all eternity, I still love you, and I will continue to love you, no matter where you have been, and no matter what you have done or what has been done to you. Maybe you allowed it into your life, or maybe it was forced on you. I AM here for you, to love you through the hurts, the pain, and the shame. If you never love or try to get to know ME, I KNOW YOU and I LOVE YOU...NO MATTER WHAT!

My name is JESUS CHRIST.

9 781958 004784